Rift

SEOUL SEARCHING

First paperback edition October 2022

Book Cover by ambient_studios

ISBN 978-1-7386639-0-3

Published by Midnight Story Press
www.midnightstorypress.com

Rift

SEOUL SEARCHING

MANA LEE

MIDNIGHT STORY PRESS

One

The day started out normal enough. Hyeri already knew the routine: pick up coffee, go to the set, and spend the day getting ordered around by a woman making ten times more money than her. She supposed there were worse jobs than being an actress's assistant, but sometimes she struggled to think of just what those jobs might be. And lately Ms. Han seemed to be annoyed by just about everything, picking apart anything Hyeri did, and always finding something wrong. It didn't make for an easy workday, but Hyeri had little choice in the matter. Money was money and her film major didn't seem to count for much on job applications. She just had to endure it for now.

"Fourteen thousand won, please."

Hyeri handed her money over to the barista. At least she meant to. Except when she opened her wallet, it was startlingly empty. She could have sworn she had at least a couple of bills in there. She opened up the flaps inside, hoping something would fall out, but nothing. So, she handed over her bank card instead. The machine made an annoying beeping noise after the barista swiped the card.

"It says it's over the limit," the barista said quietly.

For only fourteen thousand won? Hyeri sighed. She knew she shouldn't have bought such frivolous things yesterday, like food and water. She took back her card, feeling defeated. There was only one option left, and she was sure it wasn't going to work. Still, she had no choice but to try. She had to get these coffees or Ms. Han would not be happy with her. And Hyeri was already on thin ice with the temperamental starlet. She decided first she would check her bag, just in case the bills somehow fell in there.

As she rummaged around, she heard someone behind her give an exasperated sigh. She ignored it as she continued her search, hoping for a miracle. But there was no such luck. Resigned, she pulled out her credit card and handed it over, cringing at the expected outcome.

Just as she thought, the machine made an obnoxious noise again as the barista looked at her sympathetically.

"I'm sorry, it was declined," the young woman said.

"Maybe you can try again?" Hyeri asked.

She heard another sigh from behind her and someone grumbling as the barista swiped the card again. Hyeri crossed her fingers, hoping that just once she'd have some good luck.

"I'm sorry, it was declined again."

Damn.

Hyeri was trying to think of some way to bargain with the barista when she was suddenly pushed aside. A young man squeezed himself in front of her and held up his bank card. For a moment Hyeri thought he was going to offer to pay, like the handsome lead in a romantic drama, and then he opened his mouth, and all her hopes were dashed.

"Can I order?" he asked huffily. "This is going to make me late."

The barista tried to stutter a response as Hyeri just glared at the interrupter.

"Excuse me, I was here first," Hyeri told him, and she shoved him aside just as he had done to her.

"Well, it looks like you don't have any way to pay for this, so maybe you should go to the back of the line until you can sort yourself out," he replied and pushed back in front.

"Hey!" Hyeri said, elbowing him. "I do have money, I just—"

"Hyeri!" a voice called out from behind them. "Why didn't you wait for me? I said I would pay this time, remember?"

Hyeri felt relief as the face of her saviour came into view. It was Minki, her co-worker, and also her best friend. The two had gone to the same university together and just happened to get jobs on the same set.

"Minki, you don't have to..." she started, knowing it was a blatant lie, but trying to save face.

"It's no problem," he replied. "You'll get it next time. Add one more Americano, please."

He flashed his adorable smile as he handed his credit card over to the barista and Hyeri couldn't help but grin too as she saw the young employee's cheeks flush as she shyly smiled back. Minki always seemed to have that effect. No one could resist his charm. Well, except for Hyeri, it seemed. Although she acknowledged that he was a handsome man, she just didn't get flustered around him the way other girls did. From the time they met, she only ever saw him like a brother.

Although it seemed to be having an effect on the staff, Minki's smile did not, however, charm the rude man still standing to the side of Hyeri and glowering at her. And as soon as Minki had taken the receipt, the guy was already elbowing past her to the counter.

"What a jerk," Hyeri mumbled as she left with Minki to wait for their order.

"Who, me?" Minki asked.

"No, of course not," she replied. "You really saved me back there. Thank you. No, it's that guy ordering right now. He was acting like such an asshole before you came."

"The guy in the black sweater?" Minki asked, looking over. "He looks familiar somehow..."

"Oh, don't tell me he's a friend of yours."

"No, he's not. But I swear I know him from somewhere."

"Maybe a police report," Hyeri muttered.

She didn't realize she had been staring at the guy until suddenly they locked eyes. Hyeri quickly looked away as the man walked over. She was half expecting another confrontation, but instead her surly nemesis went past them to stand at the other end of the serving counter.

"What's up with your card anyway?" Minki asked, leading her from one awkward encounter to another. "Didn't you just get paid?"

"I did," Hyeri replied, "but all the money went to rent and bills. I barely have enough left for ramen."

"I told you moving to that place was a bad idea," Minki admonished. "The rent is draining you dry."

"I know, but I couldn't take living with roommates anymore. I need my own space."

"Plenty of nice one-rooms in Hongdae," Minki mused.

"I'm not a Hongdae girl."

"You were when I met you."

"Well, things change. I'm not a party girl anymore. I mean, I'm going to be thirty soon. I need to be more mature, live somewhere nice..."

"You'll be living on the streets before you're thirty," Minki replied, and Hyeri rubbed her forehead.

"Ugh, I know," she said. "I just need a little more time and then my pilot script will be ready. If the script gets picked up, I won't have to worry about rent anymore. Or getting coffees, for that matter."

Speaking of which, their orders were ready and up on the counter. Hyeri quickly grabbed her and Ms. Han's drinks and then she and Minki were on their way to the studio.

"We'd better hurry," Minki said. "The shoot's going to start soon."

The pair made their way inside with Minki parting ways with Hyeri in the halls. Minki was a camera operator and while Hyeri should have been making more money than him, she somehow found herself continuously broke while Minki managed to stay in the green. It wasn't fair. She just wanted a nice place to live, maybe a few amenities. And her meagre assistant's salary couldn't cover the cost. Not to mention the job was far from glamorous. She knew some people would have been excited working so close to celebrities, but for her the charm wore off very quickly. Ms. Han was a handful, to say the least. Her list of demands was long and her temper short. There'd been more than one occasion where Hyeri, or some poor other crew member, had been shrieked at by the actress over some trivial matter. Still, Hyeri couldn't quit. Truth be told, she loved the show they were working on, and the director was someone she looked up to. She was hoping that if she stayed involved with the project for a long time that she might get to propose her script to him. But this was just her silly little dream. For now, she just had to be the gopher.

Hyeri was knocked out of her thoughts by the sharp *click-clack* of high-heeled shoes coming steadily down the hall toward her.

"There you are, finally!" a shrill voice said. "Do you know how long I've been waiting?"

It was Ms. Han. Of course, it was. Hyeri just couldn't catch a break.

"I brought your—" Hyeri started but was interrupted before she could finish.

"Took you long enough. Jeez, what am I paying you for, really?"

Not paying nearly enough.

Before Hyeri could even offer the beverage, Ms. Han grabbed one of the coffees from her hands. Hyeri tried to protest, but the actress was already taking a sip. A sip that suddenly ended up all over Hyeri as Ms. Han spat it out in disgust.

"What the hell is this?" the actress cried out as Hyeri wiped coffee from her shirt. "How much damn sugar did you put in it? Are you trying to poison me? I told you, I'm not doing sugar right now!"

"Well, that was *my* coffee," Hyeri said quietly.

"What? Ew!" Ms. Han spat again, although this time onto the floor and not Hyeri. "Have you completely lost your mind? Why would you let me drink that? Eww disgusting..."

"I tried to tell you," Hyeri mumbled.

"What was that?"

She knew it was a mistake, but she couldn't help

herself. She was tired of always being stepped all over. Just once, she had to stand up for herself.

"You took the coffee before I could give you the right one," Hyeri said clearly, looking the actress in the eyes instead of bowing her head like a good little lackey.

"Excuse me? Are you saying this is my fault?"

Hyeri could feel herself faltering under that cold gaze. What was she doing? She had to swallow her pride if she was going to have any chance of coming out of this unscathed.

"I'm sorry," she said, but Ms. Han just made a dismissive noise.

"No, you're right," the actress said. "Who am I to criticize you, right? Well, let's see how you get along on your own, Ms. Bigshot. You're fired."

Hyeri felt like she had been punched in the gut. She had expected to be yelled at, maybe even hit, but she had never expected that Ms. Han would fire her. All because she had stood up for herself, albeit briefly. But that was more than enough to bruise the actress's ego. And she wouldn't stand for it.

Hyeri could only stare in disbelief as Ms. Han grabbed the other coffee from her hand and walked away. And just to add insult to injury, she tossed Hyeri's coffee into the trash on her way back to her dressing room.

Hyeri stood in the now empty hallway, still in shock. Her mind was reeling. What the hell was she going to do now? In a moment, her entire world had come crashing down. She could feel her dream slipping through her fingers. She felt her eyes begin to well up with tears as the reality of her situation hit her full force. She was off the show. She was jobless.

Before anyone could see her cry, she took off down the hall and ran outside where she could brood in peace. What was she going to do? How was she going to make her rent now? She'd have to beg her parents for money. How pitiful was that? She was supposed to be a grown-up. She had told them she could make it on her own in the entertainment industry. How could she disappoint them like this? All over a cup of coffee?

Hyeri hastily wiped her tears along with the remnants of coffee on her shirt. No, she couldn't be crying like this. She had to come up with a plan.

A sudden movement out of the corner of her eye caught her attention. It was a brightly coloured orange bill fluttering in the wind.

Money!

Without thinking, Hyeri went to grab for it. But the wind picked up and carried the bill further down the sidewalk. Undeterred, Hyeri followed after it. But once again, when it was just in reach, the wind floated the bill away, this time onto the road. There were few cars this early in the morning, so, after looking both ways, Hyeri ran out onto the road, ready to grab the pesky bill. But a particularly strong gust blew it out of her grasp and over the side of the overpass. Hyeri was about to give up then when she saw the bill firmly stuck inside a divot of one of the support beams. Now was her chance! Hooking her arm into one side of the overpass, Hyeri leaned over and tried to grab the money. But she was just a little short. Ignoring any reservations she might have had, she leaned further, trying in vain to grab the annoyingly out-of-reach bill.

She yelped as she suddenly felt someone's hands around her waist and strong arms pulling her back onto the overpass. She began to hit the man now holding on to her, but the stranger wouldn't let go.

"Don't do it!" the man was shouting. "Whatever the reason, don't do it! I'm sure you have so much to live for!"

Hyeri stopped hitting him as realization sunk in. This person wasn't trying to abduct her. He thought he was saving her from killing herself!

"No, no," Hyeri tried to explain. "I wasn't going to jump. I just..." She trailed off as she looked over at the bill just in time to see it float down onto the road below. "I was just trying to get that money."

She pointed below and the man looked down.

"Five thousand won?" he asked. "You were risking your life for five thousand measly won?"

Hyeri turned to face him, and her eyes went wide. It was the rude man from the coffee shop!

"You!" she exclaimed.

"You," he replied back, his eyes narrowing.

Looking thoroughly annoyed, the man let go of her.

"I should have known it was you trying something so stupid for such a small amount of money," he said.

"You don't even know me at all!" Hyeri countered.

"I know enough to see that you're obviously flat-out broke."

"Yes, and?" Hyeri snapped. "What, are you going to make fun of me for being poor? Go ahead, this day couldn't get any worse after all!"

The man looked taken aback by her words, his face softening for a moment as he stared into Hyeri's sad eyes. It was only for a split second, though, before he resumed his glowering.

"I don't have time for this," he said. "I'm going to be late."

"Yeah? That's what you said at the coffee shop, but here you are taking a stroll," Hyeri retorted.

The man snorted.

"You're one to talk. Shouldn't you be at your job, making money, instead of outside chasing after it?"

Hyeri didn't know how to respond. The wound of losing her job was too fresh. And here this jerk was just rubbing her face in it. Instead of coming up with some scathing reply she just made a frustrated noise and promptly turned to leave. She wanted to storm off, but unfortunately there were cars on the road now, so she had to wait to cross the street. The man stood beside her, also wanting to cross. She tried not to look over at him as the two were forced to wait awkwardly for a break in traffic in order to go their separate ways.

"You owe me a coffee," the man said.

"What?" Hyeri asked, refusing to look at him still.

"When I rushed over here, I dropped my coffee," the man went on. "You owe me a new one."

Hyeri scoffed.

"Do you really think I can afford to buy you one?"

"Wow, you don't even have seven thousand won to your name? You really are broke..."

Hyeri couldn't believe this guy. Thankfully, there was a lull in the traffic so she could make her getaway.

"And you're really an asshole," she replied and then she darted across the road, leaving the man behind.

She made her way straight to the parking lot after that, got in her car, and drove home. She ignored the frantic texts from Minki, asking her what happened, instead turning up her car radio and blasting angry hip-hop to distract herself from the thoughts that were swirling around in her head.

If only her life were different. If only she wasn't just another face in the crowd. Why couldn't she be someone special? Someone who things just seemed to always work out for. She tried to focus on the lyrics of the songs playing instead of those thoughts. And when she arrived home, she simply crawled into her bed and pulled the covers over her head. She was just going to sleep this whole horrible day away and wake up to a fresh start.

KATALK!

Hyeri ignored the sound of her instant messenger as

she rolled over in her bed. No, she wasn't ready to crawl out of her cocoon yet.

Katalk. Katalk katalk.

But the instant messages wouldn't stop. And then her phone was ringing too. Hyeri picked it up and looked at the caller ID. It was Minki. Of course, he was persistent.

"Yes?" Hyeri answered groggily, not in the mood for pleasantries.

"Hyeri! Finally! I've been trying to get a hold of you all day! What the hell happened this morning?"

"Ms. Han fired me."

"That's what she said, but I couldn't believe it. Why'd she do it?"

"She took the wrong coffee from me and then blamed it on me."

"What!"

Hyeri pulled the phone away, cringing at Minki's loud exclamation of surprise.

"That's right," Hyeri said. "She grabbed it from my hand before I could give her the right one, took a sip, and ended up spitting it all over me."

"No way. I can't believe that bitch..."

"Well, that's show business, right?"

"That's not right. That's just... it's not right."

"Nothing you can do now. It can't be helped."

"No, we need to get together, think of something."

"It's hopeless. I'm screwed."

"At the very least, you need to come out and drown your sorrows."

"Minki, I'm completely broke. I can't afford to drown anything."

"Don't worry about that. I'll get it."

"Minki, you can't always—"

"No arguing. You're coming out."

"Minki..."

"I said no arguing."

Hyeri groaned as she flipped the blankets off herself and sat up. She knew she could never resist an invitation from her friend.

"Alright, alright," she conceded, "but you better be able to keep up with me."

"Now that sounds like Hongdae Hyeri," Minki said with a chuckle.

"She might make an appearance..."

KNOWING she was going to get drunk, Hyeri decided to be responsible and take the subway to the bar instead of her car. Of course, she was already running late. But she was sure Minki would understand. She had to look nice for what would be her final night out for a long time. After this, there would be no fun evenings. Just ramen, cheap soju, and job searching. And of course, the dreaded meeting with her parents for help with the next month's rent. She really wasn't looking forward to that.

As she headed to the station, she couldn't help but notice how fresh the air outside seemed. It was still spring, so it wasn't hot and humid yet, but it still seemed extra crisp. Almost as if it was charged with energy. She found herself with an extra bounce in her step thanks to it. Within minutes, she was at the subway station and heading down the concrete steps toward the ticket gate and then down to the platform. The fresh air seemed to carry down into this space as well, something she didn't expect. She took a deep breath in, something else she never expected to do inside a subway station.

The subway arrived quickly and Hyeri stepped on and took a seat without much fuss. The train jerked forward roughly as it started up and Hyeri found herself almost falling out of her seat, but she paid it no mind. No one else seemed to either; everyone too lost in their own personal dramas to pay any attention to some minor turbulence that was commonplace when riding the subway. The train rolled to its next stop without any problems. But despite the smooth stop, Hyeri had a slight sense of unease. The air inside the car seemed different somehow, more like a chilled winter day than a balmy spring evening. It wasn't the temperature, though; it was the feeling. What Hyeri had thought was simply "freshness" outside felt more like electricity inside the car. Like the air was charged with something that made the hairs on her arm stand up. She had no choice but to endure it though, as the doors closed, and the train made its way to the next stop. This time, however, it was not so smooth. As the train rolled down the track, it began to shake, like an airplane heading into a storm. The lights flickered and only now did some people look up, mildly concerned.

Hyeri was more than a little concerned, but as she glanced up from her phone, her concern turned to annoyance as she saw who was standing next to the door. Of course, fate just had to play her like that. Because it was none other than the rude man from the coffee shop and her "saviour" from the overpass. As if he could feel her gaze, the man suddenly looked up from his phone and right at Hyeri. His eyes widened in surprise, but before Hyeri could say anything the train began to shake more violently and she was knocked from her seat, along with a few other passengers. Hyeri looked over at the rude guy, sure he had some snappy retort for her little tumble. But he wasn't looking at her. He was staring open-mouthed at the wall behind her.

Hyeri followed his gaze and couldn't believe her eyes. It was like something from a movie. There, running along the metal railing, was some kind of... lightning bolt. As Hyeri tried to pick herself up off the ground, she looked down the subway car and what she saw made her freeze in horror. In the next car over, there were thick bolts of bluish electricity cascading down the inside of the subway and passing through the other passengers. Everyone seemed to be frozen in time as the bolts passed through them, the electricity so strong it wouldn't allow their bodies to move. Hyeri had no time to move either as in an instant the electricity had reached her too. She gave just a small cry as one of the blue bolts passed through her body and she became frozen as well.

It surprisingly didn't hurt. Truthfully, she had thought that being electrocuted to death would have been a lot more painful. But she didn't feel any pain at all. In fact, she felt pretty good. Strong even. Like she could take on anything in this world.

Or another one.

Wait, what was that? That wasn't her thought. Well, yes, it had come from inside her, but she hadn't thought it. It was like someone else had just hijacked her brain for a moment. Just what... was that?

Hyeri had no time to ponder though as she suddenly found herself lying on the subway floor, gasping for breath, along with every other passenger. The rude guy who had been standing across from her was now sprawled over her legs, panting and trying to disentangle himself from the mass of limbs the floor had become. The subway continued calmly to its next stop, but as it reached the next station its doors didn't open. Hyeri could see the people outside on the platform staring at them quizzically through the windows as the train sat motionless. There were faint wisps of smoke coming out from the subway's display screen above the door as the screen flickered on and off. Just then, the announcement speaker crackled on.

"We... we will be making an emergency stop due to... due to technical difficulties," the conductor said, breathless. "All passengers, please disembark. And seek medical attention if needed."

The doors stayed closed for a few more minutes as Hyeri and the others picked themselves up off the floor and tried to regain their bearings. Then, after station attendants had shooed away the waiting passengers outside, they finally opened the doors and let them out.

"Medical staff are on the way. Please remain calm," one of the attendants called out.

Funny thing to say to a group of people who had just been electrocuted. Hyeri's head was spinning. What the hell had just happened? Had she really just been electrocuted? She didn't feel like it though. She stared down at her hands. They looked fine. If she had really been electrocuted, wouldn't there be some kind of marks? But there was nothing. She looked over at the station attendants. They seemed to be assessing some of the passengers who were waiting for first aid to arrive. But Hyeri didn't feel like she needed medical attention. In all honesty, she felt perfectly fine.

So, she decided to leave and walk the rest of the way to the bar instead of waiting around there. She was so tired of this horrible rotten day and all she wanted to do was meet her friend and drink until she forgot all about it. As she slunk away from the bewildered (and some frantic) crowd of passengers, she noticed the rude guy doing the same. Hyeri quickly changed her direction and opted to take a different exit, even if that extended her route by a bit. The last thing she wanted was to spend more time with that jerk.

SHE DECIDED NOT to tell Minki about what had happened. Well, not exactly. She told him about the subway breaking down and being forced to walk, but not about being electrocuted. She knew he would only worry (and probably force her to go see a doctor) and the last thing she wanted was to spend the rest of this crummy evening in the emergency room. Besides, she felt fine. Better than fine, actually. Maybe it was just the fact of having a near-death experience, but she actually felt better now than she had all day. And aside from her apparently fried hair (which she blamed on the wind to Minki), there seemed to be no ill effects of the electricity, physically.

So, she let the incident slip from her mind as she drank with Minki, downing shots of soju and munching on bar snacks, as the pair of them tried to come up with a plan to boost her finances.

"I'm just going to have to ask my parents for help," Hyeri said. "It's the only way I'll make it through the next couple of months."

"You think they'll agree to it?"

"I sure hope so. Otherwise, I'll be out on the street."

"Well, my couch is always open."

"Thanks, but I don't want to burden you."

"It's not a burden. You're one of my best friends."

Hyeri smiled as she thanked him. Minki really was so sweet. She was glad to have a friend like him. And she knew one day he was going to make some lucky girl very happy.

She was about to tell him so, feeling sentimental from the soju, but she was interrupted by her phone ringing. She didn't recognize the number, but, feeling curious, she answered it anyway.

"Hello?"

"Hello! Is this Kang Hyeri?"

"Yes..."

"It's Lee Heekyung, from the set. I heard about what happened today with Ms. Han. I'm so sorry for her behaviour."

Hyeri couldn't believe her ears. Lee Heekyung was the lead actor in their drama. She had had brief encounters with him on set before, but never as personal as this. She couldn't believe he was calling her now and even apologizing.

"Oh, thank you, Mr. Lee," she stuttered, not sure how to handle this sudden turn of events.

"Please, call me Heekyung. Anyway, I'm calling because I have a favour to ask you."

"Me?"

"Yes. I'm in need of an assistant, and I was wondering if you'd like the job."

"Your assistant? Really?"

She saw Minki's eyebrows go up as she mouthed,

"It's Heekyung," to him, almost laughing at his half-surprised, half-excited facial expression. Minki quickly scooted his seat over to Hyeri's side and leaned up against her so he could listen to the call, too.

"Yes," Heekyung continued, "I saw how well you took care of Ms. Han and I'd love for you to work with me. That is, if you're okay with returning to the set."

"Yes, yes, of course," Hyeri exclaimed, and she heard Heekyung's soft laugh on the other end of the line. "I mean, yes, that would be amenable."

She had to shush Minki next to her who was now smacking her shoulder a little too roughly in his excitement. Sometimes she wondered if he forgot she was still a girl and not one of his guy friends.

"That's wonderful," Heekyung said. "So I'll see you at the set tomorrow. I'll text you all the details."

"Yes. And thank you so much, Mr. Lee. I mean, Heekyung."

"It's nothing. See you tomorrow."

Hyeri ended the call, then let out a cry of triumph as Minki shook her happily.

"See? You don't have such bad luck after all," he exclaimed. "Assistant to Lee Heekyung, that's pretty damn good."

"It is, isn't it?" Hyeri said, giddy.

"This calls for another bottle to celebrate!"

"Oh no, Minki, I can't. I have to go to the set early tomorrow. And so do you."

"Just one more."

"I'm not 'Hongdae Hyeri' anymore..."

"Just half then. Come on, this is a special occasion. You're working with a big star now."

He was right. Lee Heekyung was much more famous than Ms. Han. He had many fans across all ages who knew him for his roles in famous dramas. He was charming, funny, and of course beautiful. That was how people described him. Not "handsome," but "beautiful." He had features that seemed to appeal to everyone, both men and women alike. Even Hyeri had been starstruck the first time she saw him on set, although she had grown accustomed to it now. Still, it was exciting to think that not only would she be back on the show she loved but working with someone like Heekyung.

"Alright," she said, "order one more bottle. But we're only having half."

OF COURSE, it wasn't half. Still, Hyeri was used to drinking a lot, so she wasn't doing too badly. But she really needed to get home now if she was going to make it to work tomorrow.

"You sure you can't stay longer?" Minki asked. "It's not even midnight yet."

"Nope. I need to catch the last subway."

"Forget the subway. Just take a taxi," Minki slurred.

"I can't afford a taxi."

"Aw, I'll pay. You can pay me back after your first paycheck from Mr. Big Star."

"Sorry, not gonna happen. You already paid for this, plus the coffees, and I don't want to owe you any more. Besides, you should get home too. You have to work tomorrow as well, remember."

"Okay, well, let me come with you at least. I feel bad letting a girl walk home alone."

Hyeri laughed.

"I think you're drunker than me. But don't worry, I'm fine. It's too far for you to go anyway."

"Not too far..."

Hyeri gave him a smack.

"I'm *fine*," she reiterated. "And you need to go home and sleep this off before work tomorrow. Or else the camera's going to be wobbling and Ms. Han will scream at you for ruining her close-ups."

"Ugh, you're right. Alright, as long as you're really fine to get home."

"I am. Don't worry about me."

THE SUBWAY RIDE BACK to her stop was thankfully uneventful. No electrical disturbances this time. In fact, if Hyeri didn't know any better, she could have sworn that the earlier incident had never even happened at all. She still didn't feel any different, except for maybe having a bit more energy, but that could have been the alcohol.

But other than that small side effect there didn't seem to be any adverse reaction to her little electrocution. Maybe her luck really was looking up.

As she stepped out of the subway station, she decided to stop at the nearby convenience store for some juice. There was no one inside the store save for the old man behind the counter. Hyeri quickly grabbed an orange juice and headed up to the front. As she set down her purchase, someone else entered the shop. She couldn't believe it. Maybe it was just the alcohol talking, but this man was stunningly gorgeous. He looked just like an actor. No, not like one. He looked just like a particular actor. That handsome one who played a prince in that popular period drama. Yes, he looked just like him. It was uncanny. Hyeri was in such shock that she dropped one of her coins as she fumbled about for her change. It rolled across the floor toward the handsome stranger who bent down to pick it up.

"Oh, thank you," she murmured, her drunk brain still in awe of this man.

"It's no problem," he replied. "But... are you walking alone?"

Hyeri's common sense had left her as she nodded.

"My house is not far from here," she replied, with even less common sense.

"It's not safe for a girl to walk home alone," the man cautioned. "Why don't I walk with you?"

Normally she would have declined, but she was still feeling happy from her job offer and in her drunkenness her reservations were gone. Plus, this guy looked just like that actor. She just had to get to know him and find out his story. Maybe this was true fate that had brought them together. Much better than the fate that kept bringing that coffee shop asshole to her. So, despite knowing better, Hyeri accepted the man's offer.

The air seemed colder as they exited the store together, but Hyeri wasn't too bothered. She was more interested in this new man than the changing weather patterns.

"I'm Hyeri by the way," she said as they walked together. "What's your name?"

"John," he replied and Hyeri was somewhat surprised that he gave her an English name.

"So, where are you from?" she asked him.

"Around here," was all he replied.

Okay, so he was being a bit mysterious. Still, that wasn't cause for alarm. Was it?

"So, you live around here?" she asked, hoping to get a bit more conversation out of him.

The man didn't look at her as he simply replied, "Yes," and kept on walking. Now Hyeri was feeling slightly uneasy. Maybe this wasn't such a good idea after all. Despite his handsome face, something about the guy just seemed off. In the bright lights of the convenience store he had seemed warm and friendly. But now he was brusque and off-putting. Like his mind was preoccupied with something else.

Even in her drunken state Hyeri could sense

something was wrong. She was starting to feel that she had made a bad decision here and needed to correct it.

"You know, you don't really have to walk me," she said. "It's probably out of your way. I can get on by myself."

"It's no trouble," the man replied.

This time he did look at her and flashed a smile. She was sure it was meant to be reassuring, but it chilled Hyeri to the bone. There was no emotion in that smile. Just teeth.

"Really," Hyeri insisted, "I'll be fine. You can go."

"No, I don't think so."

Hyeri felt the blood in her veins freeze like ice. What the hell had she gotten herself into? There was no one around this time of night, not even any cars. The street was alarmingly empty. And here she was with this guy who was increasingly creeping her out.

"You know, I think I left my wallet back at the convenience store," she said hurriedly. "I should go get it."

She turned to leave, but he grabbed her arm.

"No, you didn't," he said. "You put it in your bag. I saw."

Time seemed to stop in that moment. Hyeri knew then she had definitely made a mistake. And she knew that he knew she knew. She couldn't pretend everything was fine any longer.

"Let go of me," she said, but the man only shook his head.

And before Hyeri could react he was pulling her into the nearby alley. He shoved her roughly against the wall of the building, looming over her.

"I'll scream," she warned him, and the man just chuckled, a deep rumbling sound that seemed distorted somehow.

"Go ahead," he replied, his once normal-sounding voice now guttural and deep.

Then his mouth opened impossibly wide, revealing rows of sharp teeth. He leaned in and bit into Hyeri's neck, tearing it open and letting the blood spatter against him.

Hyeri did try to scream now, but it was no use. She knew she was done for. She had been caught by some terrible monster, a thing of nightmares, and now she was going to die here in this dingy alley. She prepared herself for the death that surely awaited her.

And then suddenly she was on the ground. She let out a scream, surprised that there was sound this time. But as he looked up, ready to fight off the monster attacking her, she was shocked to see Minki instead. That's when she realized she was no longer in the alleyway. She was on the floor of the bar. With her throat still intact.

So what the hell had just happened?

"Hyeri, what's wrong?" Minki was asking her. "What happened?"

He helped her back onto her chair, looking

concerned. Hyeri was panting hard, adrenaline still surging through her veins.

What had happened to her? Was it all a dream? Had she fallen asleep at the bar and dreamed the whole thing? No, it had felt too real to be a dream.

"I'm okay," she told Minki. "I just... had a sudden leg cramp. But it's alright now."

She couldn't think of a better excuse.

"Must have been some cramp," Minki mused. "It sounded like you were being murdered."

"I was," Hyeri thought, still confused.

Just then her phone rang. She answered it without looking at the number.

"Hello?"

"Hello! Is this Kang Hyeri?"

"Yes..."

"It's Lee Heekyung, from the set. I heard about what happened today with Ms. Han. I'm so sorry for her behaviour."

Hyeri couldn't believe her ears. It was the same. It was the exact same conversation from earlier. So what had happened to her? Had she seen the future?

As she continued on with her call, she realized that must have been it. Heekyung was saying the exact same things as before. And Minki's reaction was the same as well. Even the random girl bumping against the back of her chair on the way to the bathroom was the same. It was all the same.

As she ended the call, Hyeri couldn't share Minki's

enthusiasm for her new job. She was still coming to grips with the fact that she had seemingly just had a premonition.

The electricity.

Was that it? Had that fried something inside her brain, allowing this... power to appear?

"See? You don't have such bad luck after all," Minki said. "Assistant to Lee Heekyung, that's pretty damn good."

"It is..."

Minki's smile faltered.

"What's wrong?" he asked. "Is your leg still bothering you?"

Hyeri shook her head.

"No, it's not that," she said. "I'm just... I'm still in shock that I actually got a new job."

Again.

"Well don't be. Things are looking up for you! This calls for another bottle to celebrate!"

Once again Hyeri found herself arguing over ordering another round. Only this time she didn't give in.

"No, I really should get going," she said. "I need to be fresh for tomorrow."

"Oh alright," Minki conceded, "but let me walk with you to the station at least. I feel bad letting you walk there alone."

This time she did take him up on the offer. And as they reached the station, she made one more request.

"Do you think you could walk me to my home?" she asked quietly, fully aware of how silly it seemed, but not able to quite shake the feeling of that monster's teeth against her neck.

"Ms. Kang, are you trying to seduce me?" Minki asked playfully. "I'm not that drunk, you know."

"Very funny," Hyeri replied. "No, it's just there are a lot of creeps around and I'm a little drunk and I... I mean I just..."

"It's alright," Minki said, saving her the embarrassment of having to come right out and ask him to protect her, "I'll go with you. It's not like I'm doing anything else tonight."

"I'm sorry."

"No, I didn't mean it like that. I mean it's like I said before, you're my best friend. So where else would I be but by your side?"

Hyeri felt her cheeks flush at his sincere words. After everything that had happened, she was extremely grateful to have someone like Minki with her. Not just for the added protection, but the support as well.

"Thank you," she said warmly and Minki patted her head.

"No problem, big sister."

"Ugh, don't call me that! I'm only sixteen days older than you! You make me feel old."

"No, old would be if I called you 'ma'am' or 'Aunt Hyeri,'" Minki replied with a grin.

Hyeri gave him a playful smack.

"You better never call me either of those."

Once again it was a calm subway ride. So calm that Hyeri found herself falling asleep on Minki's shoulder. Luckily, she caught herself before she could nod off. That was just how it was being friends with Minki. His personality was so comforting that even after a stressful day she could relax next to him.

That relaxation was short-lived, however, as they soon came to her stop. Hyeri felt herself on edge as they exited the station together. Would there be a monster waiting for them? Would something else happen?

But things were thankfully normal as they walked down the busy street toward her apartment. As they neared the alleyway where she had "died" earlier, Hyeri felt herself instinctively grab on to Minki.

"Are you okay?" he asked. "You seem really spooked."

Hyeri glanced down the alleyway as they passed it, steeling herself for something terrible awaiting them there, but it was empty.

"I'm fine," she lied. "I just... I had a really vivid dream earlier. And it really freaked me out."

"What happened in it?"

"Well, I died," Hyeri said matter-of-factly. "In that alleyway."

"What? Are you serious? That's awful."

Yeah, it was.

"There was a man," Hyeri continued, "and he offered to walk me home. Then he pulled me into that alley and killed me."

She left out the part where he'd turned out to be a horrible monster. Even if she was just framing it as a dream, it didn't sound as believable then.

"No wonder you didn't want to walk alone," Minki said. "Well don't worry, I'll escort you safely. And remember, it was just a dream. No need to be afraid now."

Just a dream. Sure.

A dream that had felt exactly like real life. A dream that had predicted the exact events of the future, right down to the things that were said. A dream she apparently had in a split second while sitting in a bar with her friend, awake. Sure, maybe she could believe that.

But the sight of that monster, of those sharp teeth and that terrifyingly wide mouth... That impossibly low, otherworldly voice... She couldn't stop thinking about it.

"Minki?" she asked as they neared her house, "do you... do you think you could spend the night with me?"

"Okay, now you definitely are trying to seduce me, right?" he joked, but Hyeri remained serious.

"Today's been a really horrible day," she said. "First getting fired, then that asshole from the coffee shop, the subway breaking down, and my weird dream. I just really don't want to be alone right now. That's all."

"You know, if it was anyone else, I'd say no," Minki replied. "But since it's you..."

"I'll make it up to you, I promise. Once I get paid, we'll go out for drinks and I'll pay for everything, even your taxi home."

"Of course, you will."

Hyeri only felt herself relax slightly after they had entered the apartment with the door locked behind them. And as they watched TV together and drank a little bit more, she found herself feeling safe again with Minki next to her. Safe enough to actually fall asleep on his shoulder this time.

***

THE NEXT MORNING was a blur as the pair of them, feeling groggy and slightly hungover, hurriedly got ready for work. In the bright morning sun, the events of the previous day really did feel like a dream. Maybe that's all it was. But Hyeri had to be sure. So, while Minki was in the shower, Hyeri quickly got changed and headed outside. It didn't take long for her to reach the alleyway. She felt her heart pounding in her chest as she rounded the corner. And that heart jumped into her throat at what she saw. There, splattered across the wall and the pavement below, was a dark red bloodstain.

Hyeri quickly left the alleyway, not wanting to look at the horrible scene any longer. But her determination was set now. She knew what she had to do. She had been given that vision, this "power," for a reason. Her life had been spared for a reason. She had to stop that monster from killing anyone else.

But... how exactly was she going to do that?

Two

If Hyeri didn't know any better, she would have thought that everything was back to normal. Nothing seemed out of the ordinary as she and Minki walked to the coffee shop near the studio. It was the same as it was the day before, the shop full of the usual studio employees grabbing their morning coffees, the baristas working tirelessly to make sure cups were filled in good time. Yep, everything was normal here. But in Hyeri's world, not so much.

As she approached the end of the line, someone abruptly cut in front of her.

"Hey!" she exclaimed.

Her surprise quickly turned into annoyance when she saw who it was. It was the same rude guy from yesterday! Of course, she just couldn't escape him.

"I was here first," Hyeri said.

"No way, I'm not getting stuck behind you again,"

the man replied. "Besides, I thought you couldn't afford coffee."

"Well, I can," Hyeri replied, leaving out the fact that Minki was once again paying for it.

"Oh good," the man said, smiling sarcastically, "then you can pay for my coffee that you ruined yesterday."

He gestured for her to go ahead of him, but Hyeri just glared at him.

"I'm not paying for anything for you," she told him. "Not with your attitude."

"I saved you," the man argued. "I risked my life running across that street to pull you back."

"Well, I wasn't trying to jump, so you didn't save me from anything. Except maybe becoming five thousand won richer."

"If that bill meant so much to you, why don't you just go back outside and look for it?"

"You really are an asshole, you know that?"

"And you're just an insolent brat!"

Hyeri gasped as his final word was punctuated by another patron's coffee flying off their table and falling at her feet, splashing coffee all over her shoes.

"Oh, seriously?" she groaned.

"I'm so sorry," the other person was saying. "I don't know what happened. I didn't even touch it. It was like it just flew off there!"

He went to grab some napkins for her as Hyeri wiggled her wet toes in despair. She looked over at the rude guy, sure he would have some snarky response, but he was silent. In fact, he almost looked scared. And before Hyeri could ask him what was wrong he bolted. He just left the shop without even buying his precious coffee. Lucky for her she supposed.

"I'm starting to think you do have bad luck," Minki said as the other patron returned with a handful of napkins.

"I told you," Hyeri replied glumly.

After futilely blotting at her shoes, she and Minki ordered, grabbed their coffees, and headed over to the studio. Hyeri felt her shoulders instinctively hunch as she entered the building and she had to will herself to relax. She was so used to Ms. Han's temper tantrums, but that wasn't the case anymore. She was worried she might run into her former employer in the halls, but thankfully Ms. Han was off somewhere else. Instead Hyeri walked to Heekyung's dressing room and knocked softly.

"Come in!"

Things were bustling inside the room as the stylists put the finishing touches on the actor's look for the day. As he looked over in Hyeri's direction she felt herself once again in awe of his beauty. He had such lovely pale skin, contrasted by his long, dark black hair and deep brown eyes. His nose was long and straight, and his lips were a perfect shade of pink even without lip tint. He looked like a prince (or maybe a princess, as he was more beautiful than handsome) straight from a fairy tale.

"Hyeri, there you are," he greeted her warmly, then

addressed his stylists. "Everyone, this is my new assistant, Hyeri. I stole her from Ms. Han. Please treat her well."

The stylists gave a quick nod to Hyeri, murmuring their greetings as Hyeri bowed back to them.

"I have your coffee," Hyeri said, holding out the drink. "Vanilla latte, extra sweet."

"Oh, thank you, that's wonderful," Heekyung replied, delicately taking the drink from her grasp.

Even his hands were beautiful, with their long fingers and perfectly manicured nails. She could tell he took good care of his skin, along with the rest of his image.

"How was the drive here?" he asked her. "I hope there wasn't too much traffic."

"It was fine," Hyeri replied.

She could feel her body begin to relax more at his pleasant small talk. It was such a nice change of pace from her usual morning routine of hearing about all her perceived shortcomings before receiving a stack of orders to attend to.

"Don't worry too much about today," Heekyung said. "It should be fairly slow. I know you're used to much more fast-paced work, but that's not how I do things. So don't worry, okay?"

She could read between the lines. She knew he had on more than one occasion been witness to one of Ms. Han's outbursts. "Fast-paced" was just a nice way of saying "demanding."

"Thank you," Hyeri replied. "I won't disappoint you."

"I know you won't," he said with a friendly smile.

Hyeri relaxed even more at that. His smile was so sincere, she really could believe that he would take care of her. He was older than her, in his late thirties, nearly forty, so there was a sense of an older brother type. More so than with Minki, who was the same age as her. And who liked to pretend he was younger, even if it was only by a couple of weeks.

"There's not much to do right now, so why don't you have a seat over there," Heekyung said, gesturing to the nearby couch. "We're just about to film scene twenty-eight, but afterward we can go over my schedule and appointments."

Hyeri was surprised. Ms. Han would have never allowed her to sit, even if she had nothing to do. If the actress was standing, then Hyeri had to stand too. And if the actress was sitting, well, Hyeri still had to stand as she was usually sent on some kind of meandering errand or forced to do some useless task, just to keep busy.

She hesitated at first, not sure if she had heard him correctly. She looked over at the couch quizzically and Heekyung laughed softly.

"Yes, sit down," he urged her. "It's alright."

Hyeri tentatively sat on the couch, resting on the edge, her back straight, ready to jump up at a moment's notice. It felt like a trap. She was so used to playing mental tug-of-war with Ms. Han it was like her mind refused to believe Heekyung's words were true.

"You're really ready for the job, aren't you,"

Heekyung said, his soft laughter making Hyeri's posture relax just a little bit. "Alright then, I have an assignment for you. Read that newspaper."

He pointed to the one sitting next to her on the couch and Hyeri looked over at it. Still not quite confident, she gingerly picked it up and looked over the front page.

"Tell me if there's anything interesting," Heekyung requested.

There *was* something interesting, although she supposed it wouldn't be proper to tell Heekyung about. The front-page story was about missing girls. Missing girls who just happened to mostly be from Hyeri's neighbourhood. Five of them, all vanished with only minimal evidence left behind. The newspaper was speculating on a serial killer or sex trafficking ring. But Hyeri knew better. She was sure it was that monster from her vision. And it was still out there, lurking in the shadows, waiting to claim another innocent girl's life. As she read on, she noticed that one girl was last seen not far from their studio. Hyeri knew already that she had to investigate. She didn't know what she would find, but she had to try anyway. She owed it to whoever died in her place last night.

LATER IN THE DAY, under the guise of grabbing some takeout, Hyeri slipped away from the studio and headed out to the missing girl's last known whereabouts. The girl was last seen at a convenience store, just as Hyeri had been. Hyeri went to the shop first. She didn't bother looking around inside. She knew this wasn't the scene of the crime. Most likely the creature had devoured the poor girl somewhere else, somewhere more secluded. Hyeri shuddered at the thought. She could still clearly remember the thing's awful face, its huge mouth and soulless eyes, and those teeth tearing into her. She put a hand up to her neck, covering it as she remembered. It was all too fresh in her mind, her untimely "death."

She walked further down the street, away from the convenience store, looking for the likely murder spot. It wasn't long before she came upon a small park. She didn't know why, but she knew in that moment that it was the place. It was like something from deep within was signalling to her, something out of her control.

The park was surprisingly empty for midday. She scanned the small green area, not quite sure what she was looking for. Then she saw it. A small, discoloured patch in the dirt. She quickly went over to investigate. It didn't look that different from the rest of the dirt, but somehow, she just knew it was blood. As she bent down closer to examine it that's when she saw something shining beneath the bush. It was a small hairpin. Carefully Hyeri picked it up.

Suddenly she found her mind bombarded with images, quick flashes of things already past. She saw the girl who had disappeared talking to the handsome stranger outside of the convenience store. She saw them walking together. And the man pulled the girl into the park. Then she saw him transform once again, that handsome face contorting into something monstrous before he went in for the kill.

Hyeri screamed, flailing her arms as she fell backward onto the ground. She wasn't ready for another vision and certainly not one of someone's gruesome death. She rubbed at her head, wincing as she opened her eyes. The sight before her made her scream again. There was someone standing over her, peering down at her with an inquisitive look in their eyes.

It was the dead girl.

Hyeri scrabbled along the dirt, trying to get away, her brain desperately trying to comprehend what she was seeing.

A ghost. A ghost! It was a real, live (well not really "live," she supposed) ghost in front of her. The girl in question looked fairly ordinary. She wasn't transparent or floating, the way Hyeri expected a ghost to be. Aside from the gaping wound in her neck, and the blood splattered across her dress, she looked just like a typical young woman. She was still staring at Hyeri, but she thankfully didn't come any closer.

"Wh-what do you want?" Hyeri stuttered.

The ghost girl pointed across the park. Hyeri followed her gaze but couldn't see anything. She looked back at the ghost girl for an explanation, but the girl remained silent, her outstretched arm still pointing across the park. Cautiously, Hyeri picked herself up out of the dirt and slowly walked toward where the girl was pointing. At first, she didn't notice anything. And then something shimmered. She wasn't sure exactly what she was seeing or how to describe it. There, across one of the shrubs, was some kind of... distortion. It was as if the world was a picture and in this spot, it was torn and jagged. As though reality itself had ripped open, leaving a tear in the fabric of their dimension.

A rift.

That word popped into her head seemingly of its own accord and she deemed it the most fitting to describe what it was.

Hyeri looked back at the ghost girl who had come over now, cringing at the awful wound in the girl's neck.

"I don't understand," Hyeri said. "What is this?"

The ghost opened her mouth to speak, but no sound came out. Hyeri guessed it was an unfortunate outcome of her injury.

"I'm sorry," Hyeri said. "I can't hear you."

The ghost now made a gesture with her hands, bringing them together as if closing something.

"You want me to close it?" Hyeri asked. "How?"

Of course, the ghost did not reply. Instead, she only made the closing gesture again.

"I don't know how," Hyeri reiterated.

The ghost more insistently made the gesture, her eyes darkening at Hyeri's ignorance.

"I don't know what you mean," Hyeri said, her fear

growing as the ghost was now angrily making the gesture again and again.

"Please," Hyeri pleaded. "Stop…"

In a rage the ghost flew at Hyeri and grabbed her by the shoulders. It was only for a split second before the angry ghost vanished, but it was enough for Hyeri. With a frightened yelp she ran out of the park as fast as she could. And she didn't stop running until she made it back to the studio. There she found Minki in the halls.

"Weren't you going to get food?" he asked, eyeing her empty hands.

"Minki, I can't do this," Hyeri said. "Something really weird is going on."

"Like what?"

She wanted to tell him everything. About the subway, her vision, and now this ghost. But she realized how it would sound. He would never believe her. And he would probably think there was something seriously wrong with her. So she decided to keep her mouth shut.

"It's… it's nothing," she finished lamely. "I'm just still feeling stressed from yesterday. I just… don't feel like myself."

"Don't worry too much," Minki said. "I know yesterday was hard, but things are looking up for you."

"Sure, that's what you say."

"Excuse me," a voice from behind her said.

Hyeri moved out of the way to let the person pass. But her eyes narrowed as she saw who it was. Of course, it was her ever-present shadow, that rude guy who kept showing up everywhere she went.

"You..." Hyeri muttered.

"Oh, it's Ms. Five Thousand Won," the man replied. "I'd love to argue with you some more, but I've got a scene to shoot."

"You work here?"

"Yes, and once again you're going to make me late, so let's just end it here."

"Gladly."

And with that he continued down the hall.

"I can't believe he works here too," Hyeri complained. "I keep running into him everywhere; it's so annoying."

"I knew he looked familiar," Minki said, thinking out loud. "He works on our drama. He plays the café owner."

"What? He's on our set?"

"Yes, I'm sure it's him. His part is small, but he's in the background of a lot of scenes."

"Great, so I'll be seeing more of him."

"What is the deal with you two anyway? Why do you hate each other?"

"I hate him because he's so damn rude to me all the time. I have no idea why he hates *me* though."

"Maybe he just has a diva personality. You know, some of these background actors really let their egos get out of check."

"Maybe... I just don't understand why I have to keep

running into him. It's like the whole universe is against me lately."

Hyeri found herself feeing restless for the rest of the day. It wasn't just the rude guy (whose name was Dongwoon, she discovered). She kept expecting ghosts to pop up. Or another terrifying monster. It made her feel on edge the whole time they were filming. Worst of all, she couldn't talk to Minki about it. He needed to focus on his camerawork, and even then, she knew she couldn't tell him what really happened. Still, it was a bit of a comfort to have him there. And Heekyung too. The actor's energy was so much different from Ms. Han's. He was lively and fun, always entertaining the crew between scenes and talking freely with anyone, regardless of their social status. It was a huge departure from the ice queen that was Ms. Han. Most people avoided her unless they had to work with her directly. Which meant they had avoided Hyeri too. Although she loved the show, her time working on it had been fairly lonely. If it hadn't been for Minki, she might have been totally isolated.

"Quiet on the set!"

Hyeri stilled herself as the words rang out. They were getting ready to film the final scene of the night, a tender moment between Ms. Han's character and Heekyung's. It was amazing just how much the actress's personality changed in front of the camera. Onscreen she was the definition of the perfect girlfriend: bright, bubbly, loving and kind. Offscreen she was anything but. She was very good at acting, Hyeri had to admit.

As Hyeri watched the pair of actors pretending to be lovers, she couldn't help but feel a pang of longing. She wished she could find someone like that for herself. But these days it seemed that finding a good man was like looking for a needle in a haystack. No, she only seemed to attract guys like Dongwoon.

She grimaced as she felt a sudden pain inside her head. Great, now even the thought of that asshole was giving her a headache. The pain began to grow stronger and Hyeri wondered if she should quietly excuse herself to go take some medicine. She had no time, however, as the pain inside her head flared unbearably and then flashes of images came to her. A girl standing outside alone. A handsome man approaching her. And then razor-sharp teeth coming toward her face.

Hyeri cried out, flailing her arms against the unseen attacker as she fell back onto the ground.

The monster! It was going to kill again!

"Cut! Cut!" the director yelled.

Hyeri looked out at the crew as she came around from her momentary lapse in reality. Everyone was staring at her. She felt herself shrink back under the gaze of all their eyes.

"I-I'm sorry," she said. "I had a sudden migraine pain. I'm so sorry."

She picked herself up off the ground, embarrassed, as some of the crew came over to help her.

"Unbelievable," Ms. Han exclaimed. "That was probably my best take, and she ruined it! I knew there was a reason I fired her. Can't we throw her off the set? This is pure sabotage."

"Excuse me, but she's my assistant," Heekyung said, coming to Hyeri's defence. "And she's not going anywhere."

"She ruined the take for you too."

"And I don't care. I'd rather see that she's properly taken care of than worry about my take. Besides, I can do it just as well again. Can't you?"

"This is ridiculous," Ms. Han huffed, but Heekyung was no longer paying attention to her.

Instead, he was walking over to Hyeri, asking if she was alright. Hyeri didn't know how to answer that question. Physically she felt fine now. But mentally, she was still trying to regain her bearings. And there was no one she could talk to about any of this.

"I think I'm fine," she told Heekyung. "The pain's gone now."

"Are you sure?"

Heekyung was looking at her with such genuine concern in his warm brown eyes that Hyeri felt her heart actually flutter a little. Nobody ever looked at her like that. Not even Minki.

"I'll be okay," she lied.

"Your face is so pale," Heekyung remarked. "You look like you've seen a ghost."

It was just an expression, but Hyeri couldn't help but feel her stomach drop at his words. Heekyung must have noticed her discomfort as he reached over and took her hand in his. Then he looked over at the director.

"Can we take a short break?" he asked. "I want to make sure she's really okay."

Hyeri was about to protest, to assure him that she was fine, but Ms. Han beat her to it.

"This is unbelievable," the actress complained. "We're going to have to stop production for *her*? No, I refuse. We'll keep going."

Heekyung let go of Hyeri's hand and stood up to face Ms. Han.

"Might I remind you that this is *my* show," he said, his voice low. "And the crew listen to me. So if I say we're taking a break, then we're taking a break."

Ms. Han glared at him, but she did not argue any further.

Instead, she only smirked as she looked over at Hyeri and said, "She's not nearly as pretty as the girls you usually go for."

Then she turned and walked away, high heels *click-clacking* angrily across the floor.

"Alright, we'll have a fifteen-minute break," the director called out. "Then back to it."

Some of the crew grumbled at this sudden pause in their work and Hyeri felt bad. She didn't want to be a burden. Still, she wasn't going to argue with Heekyung.

"Let's go to my dressing room," he said. "I'll get you some water. Are you able to walk okay?"

Hyeri nodded as she shakily stood up. But even so

Heekyung held out his arm for her to take. Not wanting to offend him, she held on to it, even though she was sure she could make it on her own.

"Thank you," she said, and she really meant it. "And I'm so sorry. I'm not usually like this, but the last few days have been... stressful."

"I bet," Heekyung replied. "Getting fired is never fun."

Oh right, that. Hyeri hadn't even been thinking of that.

"It's not just that," she mumbled.

She was still trying to piece together her vision. The monster had been attacking a girl, that much was clear. But where? And when? The uncertainty was killing her. She just knew she had to help that poor girl. She wanted to talk to Heekyung about it. But she knew he would just think she was crazy if she just laid it all out for him. So, she decided to cautiously broach the subject.

"Have you... have you ever seen a ghost?" she asked.

She expected him to look at her like she was nuts, or at the very least that she was joking. But he seemed thoughtful.

"Did you see a ghost on the set?" he asked, his voice soft.

"Not exactly," she replied. "But I'm pretty sure I saw one in the park earlier."

"Really?" he asked, sounding intrigued. "What did it look like?"

"Terrifying. I ran all the way back here."

"You know, last night I thought I experienced something paranormal too."

"Really?!"

Hyeri tried to control the eagerness in her voice. She was just so relieved that she wasn't the only one having weird experiences.

"Yeah, it was while I was sleeping. I just felt like someone was watching me."

"Did someone appear to you?"

"Not really. It was more of just a feeling. Well, there was a shadow in my room, but I'm pretty sure it was just my coat hanging up."

He chuckled and Hyeri felt somewhat deflated. He was just describing things that everyone went through at some point. He hadn't seen a full-blown apparition like she had.

"Don't worry too much about it," Heekyung said. "I'm sure it was just stress causing your mind to play tricks on you."

"Yeah, you're probably right."

Or maybe it was the weird electricity that had turned her into a human crystal ball. As if on cue, she felt a sharp pain in her head again as a single image flashed in her mind.

It was a sign from a chicken restaurant. She knew right away this was near where the girl was about to be attacked. And she knew she had to stop it from happening.

"You know what, I think I need to get some fresh

air," she told Heekyung. "I'm just going to step out for a bit, if that's okay."

She quickly excused herself, then hurried down the hallway. She nearly bumped into Dongwoon on the way out (why was he always around her at the worst times?) but thankfully avoided a collision. As soon as she made it out of the building, she took off running down the street.

She had to stop it. She had to save that girl. Those were her only thoughts as she sprinted down the sidewalk. Someone else had died because of her last night. She had avoided death, but some other girl had taken her place. She couldn't let it happen again. She had to do something.

Soon enough she reached the chicken place she had seen in her vision. But where to go from there? She scanned the streets. There was no sign of the girl or the man. Which way was she supposed to go? Frustrated, she hit her fist against the restaurant's sign. And she was gifted with a vision for it. In an instant she saw the pair's route, going from the restaurant, down the street, to a secluded area in a market not far away. Everything there would be closed this time of night and there would be few people around. He must have charmed that girl into following him out there, just as he had done to Hyeri.

Without thinking, Hyeri ran down the street, hoping to catch up with the pair before it was too late. As she rounded the corner of the deserted market and dipped into one of the small alleyways, she saw she was just in the nick of time. The monster had the girl by the shoulders and was just starting to transform.

"Hey!" Hyeri yelled. "Leave her alone, you freak!"

The monster turned his attention to her and Hyeri felt her blood run cold. Once again, she was staring into those lifeless eyes, into that big, toothy mouth. And with growing horror she realized that she had no idea how to stop this thing.

"So you want to be my next meal instead?" the creature asked.

He let go of the other girl who quickly ran away with not even a thank you to Hyeri.

"Back off," Hyeri said, trying to sound commanding, but unable to keep the waver out of her voice.

"You smell so good," the monster said as he began moving closer. "Want to taste..."

Hyeri frantically looked around for something to defend herself with. She picked up a broken piece of a wooden pallet and held it out in front of her, trying to look menacing. She had no idea what she was doing. She just knew she had to stop this monster somehow.

The creature charged toward her and Hyeri braced herself for the attack. But the attack never came. Instead, several bolts of blue electricity hit the monster, knocking it backward. The electricity engulfed the creature, and it began to convulse on the ground, smoke coming out of its body. Then it was still.

Hyeri turned around to the source of the electricity and couldn't believe what she was seeing. It was

Dongwoon. He looked at the flimsy piece of wood in her hands and scoffed.

"Did you really think you were going to stop that thing with *that*?" he asked.

"What are you doing here?"

"Saving your butt apparently."

"Hey! I was just fine."

"What? You were about to be killed by that weirdo. Whatever he is..."

"And how do you know that? I could have some secret fighting power too, you know."

"Yeah, and what's that?"

"Well, I don't know yet. So far, I only get visions of the future."

"Well, a lot of good that did you."

"You know what..."

"Whoa."

Dongwoon shushed her as he noticed the creature stirring. The thing reached out to grab Hyeri's leg but then Dongwoon raised his hand to it and the monster went flying backward before landing in an empty market stall.

No way, this guy had *two* powers? Electricity and telekinesis. That just wasn't fair. All Hyeri had was her stupid visions. Well, unless you counted the ability to see ghosts, something she wasn't all that keen on.

"Stay back," Dongwoon cautioned her.

He raised his hand again and several bolts of electricity flew out and headed straight for the monster.

This time Dongwoon concentrated his energy for a longer amount of time. The monster shook and convulsed until thick black-looking blood began to come out of its horrible gaping, shark-toothed mouth.

"Is it dead?" Hyeri asked.

"I... I think so..."

"You were on the subway too that day," Hyeri mused. "When we were all electrocuted. Was that when your power started?"

"Yeah."

She wanted to ask him more, like if he knew if there were others like them, like some kind of super team, but she was rudely interrupted by a ghostly apparition appearing beside her. Hyeri cried out as the park ghost appeared and Dongwoon looked at her funny.

"What is it?" he asked, already looking annoyed with her despite the two of them having the shared experience of destroying an evil monster together.

"You can't see her?" Hyeri asked.

"See who?"

"There's a ghost trying to get our attention."

"A ghost?" Dongwoon asked incredulously. "Where?"

"Right in front of you. I guess you don't have the power to see her."

"Nope, there's nothing there."

The ghost pointed down the street, then made a closing gesture just like before.

"There's something she wants us to do. In the park

nearby. There's a tear or a rift or something. We need to close it. Somehow."

"What are you talking about?"

"I don't know. Just come and see for yourself. Oh, but don't—" Hyeri's words were interrupted by Dongwoon's surprised face, followed by his involuntary shudder. "—walk through the ghost," she finished.

"Ugh, you really are telling the truth, aren't you?" Dongwon replied, still shivering.

"Yes. Now come on."

Hyeri led him to the little neighbourhood park and showed him the rift.

"What's that?" Dongwoon asked.

"I'm not sure," Hyeri replied. "It looks like some kind of... tear in reality. Like a rip in the fabric of the universe."

"This is so weird..."

"I think it's where the monster came from," Hyeri continued. "The ghost, she wants me to close it. But I don't know how. I was hoping you'd know."

"Me? How would I know anything about this?"

"Well, you showed up suddenly with these crazy superpowers."

"Hey, I only have this... disability... after what happened in the subway yesterday. I have no idea how to fix rips in reality or whatever it is."

"Well, I don't know either, but we've got to figure out something. She's waiting for us to do something."

Hyeri looked over at the ghost warily. The girl just

kept repeating the closing gesture, looking more insistent now. Suddenly the rift began to shine more brightly. And to Hyeri's horror it began to widen.

"We've got to do something," Hyeri said. "Look, it's opening up. What if another monster comes through?"

"Well, I don't know what to do."

"Just blast it with your power or something!"

Dongwoon obediently held up his hand toward the rift, but nothing happened.

"Hurry!" Hyeri said. "Do something!"

"I... I don't know how!" Dongwoon exclaimed. "I don't have control over it yet."

"What! So you mean you could have electrocuted me back there?"

"Oh, like you're so in control of your power, screaming in the middle of shooting a scene."

"I never said I had control over mine. Besides, now is not the time!"

The ghost was becoming even more insistent now, growing angry at their inability to take care of the growing rift.

"Nothing's happening," Dongwoon said. "I can't do it!"

The ghost suddenly became enraged and rushed toward Hyeri. Hyeri yelped and grabbed on to Dongwoon. A burst of white electricity shot from Dongwoon's hand and into the rift. The rift glowed brightly for a moment and then it seemed to close back in on itself, disappearing with a *tthwp* sound. Hyeri stared in amazement at what had just happened before realizing she was still holding on to Dongwoon. She quickly let go before he could say anything to her in response. Then she sighed in relief as the ghost girl next to her vanished.

"Oh, thank God, she's gone," she said, breathily.

"Is that it?" Dongwoon asked. "Is it fixed?"

"I think so. The ghost is gone now. I think we did it."

"*We?*" Dongwoon replied. "I'm the one who closed that thing."

"Yeah, with my help," Hyeri argued. "You couldn't do anything until I grabbed you. It was my power that guided you."

"And how do you know that? Maybe mine was just charging up."

"I can't believe you're arguing about this," Hyeri muttered. "Whatever it was, it's closed now."

"Good. So that means I can get back to work and stop wasting my time talking to you."

"You're the one who keeps showing up everywhere I go," Hyeri seethed. "Hey, speaking of which, how did you know to come and find me where the monster was?"

"I don't know," Dongwoon mumbled. "I just got this sudden urge to start running after I saw you in the hall. It was so weird. When I came across you and that... thing, I figured I must have been in the right place."

"Well, thank you," Hyeri said, hating to say it. "I might have been in trouble if you hadn't shown up."

"You definitely would have been."

"You don't know that."

"Really? You were going to stop a monster like that with that little piece of wood?"

"Maybe my true power was just charging up."

"You are so full of it..."

The two of them continued to bicker as they left the park and headed back toward the studio. They were too busy arguing to notice a strange figure watching them from the shadows.

<hr>

HARU SIGHED as he watched the humans go. Were these really the hands that the fate of the world was left in?

They were surely doomed then.

Three

It was a good morning. Hyeri woke up feeling well rested for once. It had been several days since her encounter with the monster and after a few fitful nights she was now sleeping soundly. Things were starting to look up, she felt. And today was her day off too. She planned to spend it at a nice café, working on her script. She still had quite a bit of editing to do before it would be ready to pitch. She was just imagining how her first scene would look on camera when her head began to throb.

No... Not a vision. Not today.

She hadn't experienced anything psychic since that night she and Dongwoon had killed the monster. And for that she was grateful. But she knew that was all about to change now.

She winced as the pain flared up and images flashed in her brain.

A woman with a blank stare. A man asking her what's wrong. The woman drawing lazy circles with her finger on the wall while the man begged her to speak to him.

Hyeri took a deep breath in as the images faded away. That vision wasn't quite as painful as the last ones had been. Probably because no one was being eaten alive in this one. Still, it made her uneasy. There was something so unsettling about the woman's stare. Like there was nothing inside her. Just an empty husk.

Although there wasn't much evidence to support it, Hyeri knew there must be something supernatural about this occurrence. Why else would she have seen it? She wasn't sure what she could do about it though. The visions hadn't provided her with much information. She wished her newfound power didn't have to be so vague. Why couldn't she just get a clear-cut message? Like "Don't walk home with that man from the convenience store." Or better yet, "Here are the winning lottery numbers." But that was never how these things worked, was it? It frustrated her to no end.

As she lay there in her bed feeling restless, she glanced over at her phone. She wondered if maybe she should call Dongwoon. The surly actor had begrudgingly exchanged contact details with her after the last incident. The two of them hadn't talked since then, despite working on the same set, but she figured this was worth breaking their unwritten pact of silence. He was the only other person she knew who had powers like her. So who better to discuss her vision with? Without waiting for doubt to creep in she grabbed her phone and dialled Dongwoon's number.

"Hello?"

"Dongwoon, I had another vision."

"Who is this?"

"Who do you think it is? Who else has visions?"

"Ugh, not you…"

"Look, I had another vision, of something creepy."

"What time is it?"

"Are you even listening to me?"

"It's too early for this…"

"Look, something weird is going on again."

"And why are you telling me?"

"Because I figured you could help."

"What do you think I am, some kind of superhero?"

"Well… yeah, I mean, aren't we?"

Dongwoon scoffed.

"Don't be ridiculous," he said.

"Okay, maybe we're not superheroes," Hyeri went on, "but we have these powers for a reason. I have these visions for a reason. We have to stop whatever weirdness is happening."

"No."

"What? How can you just say no?"

"Look, that night was just a one-time deal. I was just doing you a favour. I'm not some crime-fighting superhero who's out to save the world."

"You were given a gift…"

"A *gift*?" Dongwoon's voice rose. "I have to be careful not to make objects fly around while people are watching. I have to wear rubber gloves to use my new computer, since I fried the last one. This is *not* a gift. It's a curse."

"You don't think I have hardships too?" Hyeri argued. "That seeing ghosts is all sunshine and rainbows?"

"Look, I'd rather not argue with you on my day off. I have to see you so much already at work."

"You're pathetic."

"I'm ending this call now. Goodbye!"

And with that Hyeri was left with silence as the call disconnected.

What a jerk. As usual. But what else could she do? She couldn't force him to like her. Even if they were seemingly the only two people in the world with superpowers. She would have thought that would have brought them together. Like the two leads in a popular TV drama. Those kinds of things were always happening in those programs. But not him. He seemed even more determined to push her away now. Things weren't fair. Why did he have to hate her so much? She never did anything to him. He was the one always getting involved in her business. She guessed some people were just like that. A diva, like Minki had said.

She tried to shrug it off as she went about her morning routine. It was hard though when she began having more visions. It seemed that every step of the way was plagued by them. While having a shower she got the image of a man staring off into space. Not the greatest thing to suddenly see while naked and soaping up. While she was eating her breakfast, the image of a different man sitting motionless on a bench came to her next. And while getting dressed the image that showed up in her brain was just an empty black void. That one scared her the most. She didn't know why, but something about that pitch-blackness, that emptiness, was incredibly unnerving. Still, she couldn't figure out what it all meant. Who were these people? What was afflicting them? And how was she supposed to stop it?

It was these questions that swirled around in her head as she made her way to the subway station. Her favourite café was a ways away from her new apartment, so she decided to take the subway there since she needed to save her gas money for running errands for Heekyung. She was a little bit nervous getting on the subway again after what happened last time. Every bump and jostle made her wonder if she was going to get zapped again. Thankfully, that was not the case this time. Hyeri relaxed slightly as the train rolled along smoothly toward its destination. She put her headphones on and began to listen to her music. It put her at ease hearing the catchy pop beats. Now she just needed to concentrate on her scriptwriting. Soon she would be at the café, and she could forget all about ghosts and visions and focus on her passion, writing.

The train was not too crowded today so there were

many empty seats. But for some reason someone decided to sit right next to her instead of across the way. Hyeri didn't think much of it (there were always weirdos like that) until the stranger's arm brushed against hers and a cold chill ran up her spine. Hyeri froze for a moment, the hairs on the back of her neck standing up. She carefully hit the pause button on her music. Then she looked to her right. She screamed and jumped from her seat at what she saw. It was the ghost of a teenage boy. At least that's what she thought. His body was horribly mangled and covered in blood, his face sagging and drooping. He had an old-fashioned haircut and from what she could make out of his school uniform it looked vintage as well.

In an instant the image of a group of teenage boys beating another one flashed in her brain. Hyeri ran to the subway door, wanting to get as far away from the ghost as she could. And when the door opened seconds later, she rushed out, only looking back when she was a safe distance away on the platform. The ghost was standing up now, staring at her through the window. He waved a bloody hand at her and attempted a smile, his drooping mouth contorting into more of a grimace.

Hyeri turned and ran away. This was not a case she could help. She knew from the clothing and hairstyles of those in her vision that this happened a long time ago. So why did she have to see it? Why did these ghosts have to come to her?

As she exited the station, she was close enough to her café that she could just walk there. But she didn't want to go there now. How could she just sit down and sip a latte, like nothing had happened? There was somewhere else she needed to stop first. As she hurried down the street, she thought about what Dongwoon had said. How their powers were a curse, not a gift. She was starting to think he was right.

As she passed the rows of Buddhist shops lining the street, she began to feel a little calmer, though no less upset. Seeing the charms hanging up outside and the miniature statues sat in rows inside the windows of the shops felt somewhat reassuring.

She was done with this. She didn't want this power. And she knew what she was going to do.

Her destination soon appeared before her. The temple.

It was not too busy as she entered the grounds, with just a few practitioners making their way inside. Hyeri didn't bother to follow them through the side door. She had no time to take off her shoes, find a pillow, and prostrate herself, bowing over and over. Instead, she walked to the large open front windows facing the courtyard and stood in view of the giant golden Buddha statue housed inside the building. She bowed deeply to the statue and then she began to pray. She had never been a particularly religious person, but she figured the benevolent Buddha would help anyone in need.

"Please take this power away," she prayed fervently. "Please take this power away..."

"Take it away? Why would you want that?" a voice from behind her asked.

Hyeri jumped slightly at the sudden intrusion into her prayers. She steeled herself for another terrifying sight, sure that the owner of the voice was another ghost. But when she turned to look, it was just a normal young man staring back at her. Well, normal except for his silver hair and extremely pretty, yet cute, babyish face. He looked like a pop idol straight out of a music video. But Hyeri wasn't convinced.

"Are you... alive?" she asked cautiously.

The young man chuckled before answering, "Yes."

"So you're not a ghost?"

"No. I'm Haru. Now tell me, why do you want to give up your power? It was destiny after all, that you were chosen."

Hyeri's relief at finding out he was alive was cut short by those words. How did he know what she had been doing? What she had been thinking? Before she could even ask the question, he had an answer.

"I'm a god," Haru said. He smiled at her, a cheeky little grin that seemed far too cute for someone claiming to be an almighty being. "Well, not one from your world. Not like..." He gestured to the golden Buddha statue inside the temple. "I'm from another world."

"Huh?"

It wasn't the most eloquent of replies, but it was all Hyeri could muster. This was too much for her brain to handle. First visions, then ghosts and monsters and now gods? What, was she living inside a movie?

"You've noticed some weird stuff going on lately, haven't you?" Haru went on.

"That's an understatement."

"I'll try to explain as best I can. Most of the time our worlds sit parallel to each other, never touching or interacting. Completely independent of each other. Sometimes they graze each other, and the barriers become thin, thin enough for beings to cross over. This is a normal part of our coexistence. Most 'unusual' occurrences in your world's history can be attributed to these instances. But something happened recently that smashed our two worlds together and caused all these cracks. Rifts. Now my world is slowly bleeding into yours."

"So I was right," Hyeri mused. "That rift in the park was where the monster came from."

"Yes. And more will keep coming unless you can close them all up. Creatures more terrifying than you can imagine. And powerful too."

"But I can't close them by myself," Hyeri lamented. "I need Dongwoon to help. And he wants nothing to do with me."

"I'm sure you'll think of something," Haru replied with another cute smile.

Hyeri had more questions for him, many more, but was interrupted by her phone ringing. She looked at the caller ID. It was Heekyung, so she knew she had to take it.

"Hyeri, hello. I'm sorry to bother you on your day off, but I have a favour to ask you, if you're not busy."

"I'm not busy," she said. "I'm just hanging out at a café today."

"Oh, that's good then. I just needed someone to run through some lines with me tonight, maybe pick up some dinner along the way? I'll reimburse you of course."

"Sure, that's no problem," Hyeri said cheerily.

Truth be told she was happy to spend the evening with Heekyung instead of alone. She couldn't stop thinking about her visions, those images of emptiness. She'd rather have something to distract her instead of sitting in her big, empty apartment all by herself.

"Alright, let's meet at my place at seven then," Heekyung went on.

"Alright, see you then."

As she hung up the phone, Hyeri turned back to face Haru. But he was gone. She had been so engrossed in her phone call she hadn't noticed him leave. She scanned the grounds, looking for that silver hair among a sea of black-haired temple-goers, but she didn't see him anywhere. It was like he had simply vanished. Great, the one person who could help her out with her visions and he had disappeared before she'd even gotten a chance to ask. She looked back at the spot he had been standing in, wondering if he had even been real or just a figment of her imagination. There, in the very real footprints in the dirt, something was glittering. Hyeri bent down to pick it up. It was a necklace with a silver sun-shaped pendant. She turned the pendant over in her hand. It was smooth and unmarked, with no insignia on the back. She didn't know why, but the sight of it made her feel a little better. It was like the object itself had a calming energy. When she looked at it, she felt stronger, more assured.

And it felt so natural when she put it around her neck. Like this was where it belonged all along.

She quickly tucked it under her shirt, looking around to see if anyone saw. No one was paying attention to her. That seemed to be the case most of the time now. Everyone was too involved in their own lives to care what one random girl was doing. She supposed it made it easier when dealing with strange or spooky occurrences. But it didn't make her feel any less lonely. At least the mysterious Haru had offered some insight into her situation. So she wasn't completely alone. And she still had Minki and Heekyung, even if she couldn't tell them exactly what was going on.

She turned to face the Buddha statue once again and gave a final deep bow.

"Alright, I won't wish my powers away," she thought. "If it's destiny, then I just have to face it. But I just wish I could have a little more help…"

And with that she left the temple and headed toward the café.

SHE TRIED to focus on her writing while sipping her latte, but it proved too hard for her. She kept thinking about her visions. What did they mean? What were they trying to warn her about? Though they were all in different settings, with different people, they seemed to be all connected by a common thread. That feeling of emptiness. She hadn't just seen it; she had *felt* it too. A big, gaping void that filled her with unease. Something had happened to those people, to make them empty inside. But what? She spent more time wondering that than working on her script and soon enough the day was done, and she was supposed to be picking up food and going over to Heekyung's.

With a sigh, she packed up her woefully unfinished script and went back home to get her car. Heekyung lived across town, and it would be far too much of a hassle to take the subway all the way there and back again. Besides, she wanted to stop at her favourite *tteokbokki* restaurant along the way. She loved the squishy rice cakes simmered in a spicy sauce and she knew Heekyung was a fan too.

She was wary as she drove alongside the Han River, worried that more ghosts might pop up. Plenty of people committed suicide by jumping off one of the many bridges crossing the river and plunging into the frigid waters below, so she was sure there was no shortage of wandering spirits about. Thankfully though, none of them approached her car as it smoothly made the drive over to the eastern part of town.

She was buzzed in by a security guard as she arrived at the front gate of the apartment tower block and drove down into the visitor parking. There, she was greeted by a doorman who showed her inside the lobby and to the elevator.

Once inside the elevator, alone, she felt a bit creeped out. This was always where something scary happened in movies. As the elevator steadily made its ascent, she thought of the loving gaze of the Buddha statue that had been looking down at her at the temple earlier that day. She kept that image in her head as she stared down at her feet, not daring to look anywhere else. Luckily for her there were no ghosts in the building, and she arrived at Heekyung's floor un-accosted. Feeling lighter, she walked down the hall and knocked on the door.

"Hyeri! Welcome! Come on in."

Heekyung's smiling face greeted her from the doorway as he ushered her inside. He was dressed far more casually than she would have imagined, in a T-shirt, tracksuit bottoms and slippers. He offered Hyeri a pair of slippers in the entranceway, a nice powder blue, that clashed in contrast with his bright red ones.

"I brought *tteokbokki*," Hyeri said, holding up the takeout bag as she slipped on the slippers and followed Heekyung into the living room. "It's from the best place in town. At least in my opinion. And Minki thinks so too."

"Minki?"

"The camera operator on our set. He's also my friend."

"Oh, that Minki? He's so handsome, isn't he? He should really be in front of the camera, not behind it."

"That's what everyone seems to think," Hyeri said with a chuckle. "But he's a terrible actor. He's much better suited to behind the scenes."

"So he's your friend, is he? Not your boyfriend?"

"Oh no, no. That's another thing everyone seems to think. But I've always just seen him like a brother. We're the same age and went to the same university."

"So you're close? It must be nice to have a friend like that on set..."

His tone was wistful with just a hint of longing in it. Hyeri wondered if maybe he was lonely. She knew how the entertainment industry could be. How behind the pretty faces and warm smiles entertainers could be highly guarded, often isolated people. You never knew who was a true friend and who was only chasing fame and fortune. She supposed it was somewhat simpler being broke like she was. At least she knew Minki wasn't in it for the money.

Hyeri looked around the living room as Heekyung prepared the dining room table. It was somewhat how she had pictured it. Everything stark white and shining. White walls, white floor, white curtains, white couches. This was what the upper class considered chic. While Hyeri considered it a cleaning nightmare. She suddenly wished she hadn't brought *tteokbokki*. The thought of that bright red sauce splattering across all that white was giving her anxiety.

"Are you sure it's alright to eat *tteokbokki* in here?" she asked. "It's just so…"

"Cold? Institutional?"

"I was going to say 'clean.'"

"Ah, don't worry about that. I feel like a *tteokbokki* stain might brighten the place up," Heekyung joked. "One of the stylists helped me to decorate, told me all white was 'in.' To be honest, I'm not that fond of it. But I can't figure out what to change it to. What's the colour scheme in your apartment?"

"Mismatched," Hyeri replied. "Basically, whatever I could find for cheap."

"Ah, right."

Heekyung seemed slightly sheepish and Hyeri felt bad. She hadn't meant to shove her poverty in his face when he was just asking an innocent question.

"I think some blue would look nice," she offered, "or maybe some browns."

"You know, you might be onto something."

Dinner went surprisingly well. She had been worried beforehand that things might be awkward given their professional relationship, but Heekyung's easygoing personality put her at ease, and she soon found herself talking candidly about her past, as well as her plans for the future.

"I've almost finished my pilot script," Hyeri told him

proudly. "It's just getting it into the right hands after that."

"That sounds exciting," Heekyung said.

"More like a lot of extra work," Hyeri admitted. "I'm still editing it and that's the hardest part."

"Well don't give up. I have faith you can achieve your dream. Everyone has that power inside them; they just need the right tools to make it happen."

"Power inside them." It took Hyeri out of the moment as she thought about those words. What would Heekyung think if he knew she had a real "power" inside of her? She just hoped she wouldn't receive a vision while here in his apartment. Especially while they were eating. She didn't want to accidentally fling *tteokbokki* sauce all over his nice, white walls.

Soon enough the food was finished, and that's when the script came out. Hyeri found herself playing various parts alongside Heekyung's character, "Minchul." They played out some scenes several times, with Heekyung giving different takes on the character's emotions, sometimes asking Hyeri to change as well. She felt flattered when he asked for her feedback a couple of times. And he actually seemed to listen to her advice.

As she flipped through the script, she noticed one scene they hadn't done yet. It was short and not of much significance, but there was something on the page that caught Hyeri's eye. It said, "café owner." That was Dongwoon's part. And it looked like he finally had a few lines after a week of background work. Still, it was pretty paltry compared to other characters.

"Do you know Dongwoon well?" Hyeri asked and Heekyung seemed puzzled.

"Dongwoon?"

"The guy who plays the café owner."

Heekyung still seemed puzzled even with her explanation. And then a look of recognition came over his face.

"Ohh, him. No, I don't know him at all. I don't think we've ever talked outside of our scenes. He keeps to himself mostly, doesn't he? Very quiet and serious. Why do you ask?"

As much as Hyeri wanted to complain about Dongwoon and his horrible attitude, she had another plan in mind. One that might get him to stop hating her. Or at the very least, give her a little respect.

"He's a really great guy once you get to know him," she lied. "And I know he can act. Is there any way you could get him a bigger role?"

Heekyung smiled.

"Ah, so you have a crush on him..."

"What? Nooo... I just think he deserves more than a character with only three lines."

"So you're just doing this out of the goodness of your heart then?" Heekyung asked, raising a suspicious eyebrow.

"Yes," Hyeri lied again.

She hated being dishonest with Heekyung, who

seemed like such a genuinely good person, but she knew the truth would most likely see Dongwoon punished rather than rewarded and that was not what she needed right now. As much as she may have wanted it. They had to learn to work together if they were going to close up these rifts.

"Well, since it's you asking, I'll see what I can do," Heekyung said.

Hyeri felt her cheeks flush at those words. She didn't know why she suddenly felt so warm.

"Thank you," she said. "Um, so ready for the next scene?"

"Sure. It's Minchul and Yua in the rain, outside the café."

Hyeri gulped. So far, their scenes together had been mainly dramatic. But this one seemed like it was going to be a little more... loving.

"Alright, so I'll be Yua then," Hyeri said, mentally preparing herself.

"Well, yes, generally I play Minchul," Heekyung replied with a wry smile and Hyeri mentally smacked herself at her awkwardness.

"Right. Of course. Okay, I'll start then?"

"From here."

Heekyung pointed to a spot further down the page and Hyeri nodded. She cleared her throat and then began her best impersonation of Ms. Han.

"So you're just going to leave like that?"

"It's not what you think..."

"Then explain it to me. Minchul, please, just tell me what's going on."

"If you knew what my family was capable of..."

"I don't care! I... just want to be with you."

Hyeri felt her body grow warmer as she spoke those words.

"Yua..."

She looked up from the page and instantly regretted it. Heekyung was looking at her with such love in his eyes, so committed to his role, that Hyeri felt her heart flip-flop in her chest. He really was so beautiful, even up close like this. Even wearing such casual clothes and clashing slippers. For a moment she found herself lost in his eyes.

"Um, it's your line," Heekyung reminded her.

"What? Oh, right. Sorry. 'Minchul, don't say this is goodbye...'"

"Don't think of it as goodbye. Let's just say 'see you tomorrow.'"

"But..."

Hyeri trailed off. It was the end of her line. Because the next note in the script was "Michul kisses Yua tenderly." Hyeri looked over at Heekyung. He wasn't gazing into her eyes now. Instead, her was staring at her mouth, leaning in slightly. Hyeri felt her breath catch in her chest as her heart began to beat faster. Was he really going to kiss her? She wondered if he was a method actor.

"And then we would kiss," Heekyung said matter-of-factly. "Obviously, we don't need to rehearse that part."

Hyeri blinked, willing her heart to be still. That was intense.

"Right," she said lamely, unable to come up with any other response.

"So how was it?" Heekyung asked, oblivious to her inner turmoil. "Did it look good? Or did it make you cringe?"

No, she definitely hadn't been cringing.

"It was good," she told him. "Really good."

She wondered how he could manage to look at someone like Ms. Han like that. He really was a great actor. So good that Hyeri still found herself feeling flushed even though they were sitting far apart now. This was getting to be too much. She needed to compose herself.

"Where's your bathroom?" she asked and Heekyung pointed her down the hall.

Once inside she splashed some water on her face, hoping to cool down her burning cheeks. She splashed a little too vigorously though and caused some of her mascara to run. She delicately blotted at her eye with a tissue, then went to throw it away. That's when she noticed the other tissues in the trashcan. They were dark with bloodstains. It might have frightened her had she not known how hard Heekyung was working for their drama. Most likely he had gotten a nosebleed from the stress. The poor guy. He took his acting so seriously.

Hyeri looked in the mirror at her own reflection in dismay. She should have been working hard on her script too. Instead, she was worrying about saving people from monsters. As she stared disapprovingly at herself, she noticed a large crack in the mirror, near the top. She had the most curious urge to touch it. The more she looked at it, the stronger the urge became. As if someone (or something) was beckoning her to do it. She reached out her hand but then stopped herself. No, touching random things was how ghosts appeared, like that hairpin in the park. She'd rather not take the chance. She'd never forgive herself if she burdened Heekyung with a ghost. So she left the broken mirror alone and headed back into the living room.

The rest of the night passed uneventfully and soon enough Hyeri was back home.

But as she lay in bed later, drifting off to sleep, she couldn't help but think with a certain kind of dread what would have happened if she had touched that crack in the mirror.

Hyeri was tired the next morning as she made her way to the coffee shop. She knew she had been dreaming the night before, but for the life of her she could not remember any of it. She supposed it was for the best. She was already distracted thinking about her visions. She didn't need any more on top of that.

"Hyeri, wait!"

It was Minki, jogging up to her. Seeing him made

her feel comforted somewhat. With all the strange things going on lately it was nice just to see a familiar face.

"Just the person I was looking for," Hyeri said. "I'll buy your coffee today."

"Yeah? What, did you win the lottery?"

"Not quite. I called my parents and got a small loan from them. So coffee is on me today. And next time we go out to eat it's on me too."

"Well, thanks," Minki said. "I look forward to it. Let's eat Hanu beef and drink champagne!"

Hyeri gave him a playful smack.

"I said it was a *small* loan. I'm not rich, you know."

"Alright, alright. Pork belly and soju then," Minki conceded.

Hyeri gave him a look.

"Ramen and a shared beer?" he suggested and Hyeri nodded.

As they made their way to the coffee shop an older man roughly pushed past them, his elbow jabbing into Hyeri as he pushed between the pair.

"Hey!" she exclaimed.

"How rude," Minki muttered.

Hyeri turned around to scold the old man, but before she could she was hit by a vision. The image of a man sitting on a bench once again flashed in her mind. She realized it was the same person. The clothes, the hair, they were exactly the same. He was still shuffling down the street, bumping into other people. Then he turned and stepped out into the road. Hyeri gasped as he began to walk right into traffic.

"Hey! Stop!" she yelled.

She ran over to the man and grabbed him by the back of the shirt, pulling him back onto the sidewalk just as a bus went careening past. The pair of them fell back onto the pavement as Minki came rushing over.

"What happened?" Minki asked.

"Are you trying to die?" You almost got hit by that bus!" Hyeri yelled at the man, half angry, half relieved.

She turned to look at the man and suddenly felt sick. There was nothing behind his eyes. No intelligence, no spark of life, no dreams. Just emptiness. As Hyeri stared into his lifeless eyes, the man's attention suddenly seemed to focus on her.

"Light," he mumbled. "Light..."

He reached out to touch Hyeri's face, but Minki smacked it away.

"Is he drunk?" Minki asked, pulling Hyeri back and helping her to her feet.

"I... I don't know," Hyeri replied.

A few people had stopped now, curious about the commotion. The man was still down on the ground. He hadn't bothered to stand up, and it was attracting people's attention.

"Light..." he repeated, and he reached out for Hyeri again.

Once again Minki pulled her away, protective of his friend.

"We should go," he said. "Let someone else take care of him. We'll be late if we hang around here."

"Yeah," Hyeri mumbled, and she let Minki lead her away.

Truthfully, she was grateful to leave. She wanted to know more about her visions, yes, but something about that emptiness frightened her so much. She couldn't bear to look at it any longer. And the way the man had been reaching for her, she felt as though something terrible might happen if he were to grab on to her. So she let Minki take her away.

"That was a close call," Minki was saying. "How can people be drunk at this time in the morning?"

"He doesn't know," Hyeri thought to herself. "He couldn't see what I saw. That nothingness..."

"Are you okay?" Minki asked her. "You seem shaken up."

"Huh? Oh, I'm fine."

She turned to look back down the street. Someone had helped the man back onto his feet. He was staring off into space again, looking in Hyeri's direction with those unseeing eyes. He no longer had the fixation he had when he had been closer to her. She must have been too far away now to catch his interest.

"Come on," Minki said, ushering her inside the coffee shop. "I'm sure he'll be fine once he sleeps it off."

"Yeah, you're probably right."

She knew the truth though. That no amount of sleep would be able to shake off the stupor the man was in.

Still, she had work to do. She had to think about taking care of Heekyung now and finally making some money. There was a balance to be had between saving the world and keeping her job.

SHE DIDN'T SEE Dongwoon until later that evening. Normally she would have liked to avoid him, but this time she wanted to see him. She knew she should wait until she had some concrete news, but she was so desperate for them to get along that she wanted to tell him right away. When there was a break in filming one of the café scenes she sidled over to him, eager to put her plan in motion.

"I have some good news for you," she said as she approached him.

"You're moving away?"

"Ha ha, very funny. No, it's about your role."

"Oh yeah? And what's that?"

"I have it on good authority that your line count is getting upgraded."

"What? How do you know that?"

Hyeri knew she should remain anonymous, but she couldn't help but want a little recognition.

"I put in a good word with Heekyung," she told him. "You know how respected he is by the crew. I'm sure he can persuade one of the writers to widen your role a bit."

She thought his expression might change at that, but it remained as stony as ever.

"You're kidding, right?" Dongwoon asked.

"Nope," Hyeri said, grinning. "You're welcome."

"I wasn't thanking you."

"Eh? And why not?"

"Because I don't need your charity!" Dongwoon hissed, careful not to raise his voice too loudly in front of the crew.

Hyeri felt the grin disappear from her face.

"What? No, it's not charity," she tried to explain.

"I don't need you begging actors to get me a bigger role," Dongwoon went on. "They're going to think I put you up to this."

"No, Heekyung knows it's not like that..."

"Look, just do me a favour and stay away from me, alright?"

"Dongwoon..."

"Just go!"

"I..."

Hyeri trailed off as she felt the dull ache in her head. She put a hand up to her forehead as the ache turned into a more severe pain and she was hit with images. Once again it was people with empty looks in their eyes. Then a pair of fangs, close to her face. The last image was the only helpful thing. There was a street sign in the background. And she could actually make out the words. She knew where this was; it was close by. And she knew she needed to go there at once.

"Dongwoon, it's at the Han River Park, near the bridge," she said, still holding her forehead as the pain began to recede.

"What?" Dongwoon asked, seeming not the least bit concerned.

Hyeri lowered her voice.

"I just had a vision. Whatever the thing is that we're supposed to stop, it's at the river."

"I don't know what you're talking about."

He looked away from her defiantly.

"The visions, the ones I told you about yesterday."

But Dongwoon was unmovable.

"I thought I told you to leave me alone," was all he said.

"Fine. You want to play it that way, I'll go by myself. Just don't be surprised if you see me as a headline tomorrow."

Hyeri quickly talked to Heekyung, telling him it was a "family emergency," then left the studio. Once again, she took off running down the street, this time toward the Han River.

It was eerily quiet when she got there. It must have been still a little too cold for picnic-goers to be out yet. Hyeri scanned the grounds, not quite sure what she was looking for. Her heart was thudding in her chest, her adrenaline surging. Now that she had come all this way, she was apprehensive. What if there was another monster? How would she fight it alone? She felt the skin on her arms break out in goosebumps in the cool night air. She was beginning to feel a little scared now. Then she saw him. One of the men from her visions, standing on the bridge. He was just staring out into the park blankly, not moving at all. Hyeri quickly made her way down the path along the river's edge and climbed the steps to the bridge overhanging the park. She approached the man slowly.

"Excuse me," she said, but the man did not stir at the sound of her voice.

She called out again, but still no reaction. It wasn't until she was right next to him that the man finally looked at her. A look of recognition seemed to dawn on his otherwise expressionless face as his eyes became fixated on her.

"Light," he mumbled.

It was just like the man from earlier that day. The same blank stare, except when she got close. They both talked about "light" too.

"Excuse me, can you tell me your name?"

The man didn't respond. Instead, he reached out his hand to touch her. Hyeri backed up, just out of his grasp.

"Light," he said again.

"What happened to you?" Hyeri asked. "What did this to you?"

"Light," the man said more insistently, and he reached for Hyeri again, causing her to back up even more.

"What do you mean?" she asked. "What's this 'light' you keep talking about?"

"Liiiight," the man repeated, his words becoming a guttural growl.

Then his expressionless face grew angry and feral. He leaped at Hyeri with a growl. Hyeri jumped backward and luckily evaded his grasp once again. She turned to run, and that's when she noticed two more people right behind her. They also had ferocious looks on their faces as they wailed, "Liiiight."

Hyeri ducked under their grabbing arms and ran toward the bridge's stairs. If she got far enough away, if she could hide somewhere, she was sure they would lose interest, just as the man earlier today had. They were faster now though. Like sharks drawn to blood, they were focused on her with predatory intent. One of the women reached out to paw at Hyeri and her fingers caught on Hyeri's jacket, pulling her off-kilter. Hyeri stumbled and lurched to the right, her momentum carrying her forward and straight for the staircase. She knew in that instant she was going to fall right down all those steps and there wasn't a thing she could do to stop it. She braced herself for the impact with the metal.

But instead, someone grabbed her around the middle with one arm and used the other to push back her pursuers. Hyeri looked up, expecting to see Dongwoon. Instead, an unfamiliar face greeted her. He was handsome, with a long, sharp nose and dark, intense eyes. He was dressed in all black, in an old-fashioned outfit that would have fit right in in the Goryeo era, with shoulder-length black hair that was wild and untamed.

"Why do you smell like that?" he asked her, his voice deep and commanding.

Hyeri had no time to answer as the stranger noticed the sun pendant around her neck. It had come out from under her shirt in the scuffle. Suddenly the stranger's face began to change. His eyes went from dark brown to golden, the pupils constricting like a cat's eye. His blunted canine teeth elongated into sharp fangs that he bared angrily.

"Where did you get that necklace?" he demanded, his grip on Hyeri tightening.

Four

"Where did you get it?" the stranger repeated, snarling as Hyeri tried to twist away from him.

"Let me go!" she cried out.

And he did. Although not of his own volition. Someone had tackled him to the ground. Hyeri was surprised to see it was Dongwoon. Once again, he had come to her aid in the nick of time. The stranger easily pushed Dongwoon off him and stood up, squaring off. Dongwoon raised his hand and a small glimmer of electricity crackled along his palm. He seemed apprehensive though. There were still cars crossing the bridge and people might see him using his power. The stranger had no apprehension, however, as he reached behind himself, grabbing the handle of a blade that was sheathed across his back. Hyeri saw Dongwoon tense up, ready to fight.

"Enough!" a voice rang out.

Hyeri turned toward the sound. It was Haru, striding toward them.

"Kiha," Haru said, addressing the stranger, "put your sword away. Don't you know who they are?"

"Humans," Kiha replied. "Unusually powerful ones. And this little one's a thief too. Look at her necklace."

"She's not a thief," Haru said. "I gave her that necklace."

"Why?"

"Because she's its rightful owner. Take a good look at her. Smell her again."

Hyeri watched as the mysterious Kiha sniffed the air in her direction. His eyes widened in shock.

"It can't be..." he murmured.

"Okay, who are you people?" Dongwoon asked. "What the hell is going on?"

"Um, guys, before that, don't you think we should deal with *them*?" Hyeri asked, pointing to the expressionless people sitting on the ground. They hadn't bothered to stand up since Kiha had knocked them back into each other. Instead, they simply sat on the sidewalk, content to just stare off into space. It was hard to believe they had been intent on attacking Hyeri just moments before.

"It looks like the Soul Eater's work, doesn't it?" Haru said to Kiha as he approached.

"The *what*?" Dongwoon asked. "Really, what is going on here?"

Haru smiled at him, that cute baby-faced smile that belied his years.

"I'll explain it to you like I did to Hyeri," he said. "I'm a god, from another world. A parallel universe if you will. Something happened and our worlds collided, fragmenting them. Now rifts keep opening up and letting monsters from our world into yours. Only you and Hyeri have the power to close the rifts."

"Oh," Dongwoon said quietly, "okay."

Hyeri was livid. What? Just, what? She had been trying all week to get Dongwoon to hear her out, and he had just ignored her every time. But suddenly some random guy proclaims to be a god and he just accepts it, no questions asked?

"What the hell!" Hyeri exclaimed. "You wouldn't listen to me, but you'll take the word of someone you just met?"

"Yes, because I don't like you," Dongwoon explained as Hyeri fumed.

"Unbelievable," she muttered.

She turned away from him to look back at the people who had attacked her. They seemed docile now that they weren't focused on her anymore. She watched as Kiha knelt down to look at them. The people ignored him as they simply stared blankly into space.

"What happened to them?" Dongwoon asked.

"It looks like the Soul Eater got to them," Haru said. "It's a creature from our world. It sucks out a person's soul and eats it, leaving behind just an empty shell. It's usually not this voracious though..."

As Dongwoon neared the people they began to stir.

"Light..." one of the women murmured as she focused her attention on Dongwoon.

"Don't get too close," Hyeri cautioned. "They go berserk when they're near us. It must be our powers or something."

She noticed Kiha's expression change at that, from quiet brooding to sudden interest.

"What should we do about them?" Dongwoon asked.

"There's nothing you can do," Haru replied. "Their souls have been eaten. There's nothing inside them anymore. They're just meat."

Hyeri shuddered at his choice of words. It was so cold and uncaring. Haru looked so cute and innocent, but there was something almost sinister about his tone.

"So that's it then?" she asked. "They're just gone?"

"Well, there is one way," Haru said. "If you can find and kill the Soul Eater, you should be able to restore their souls."

Kiha snorted at that, looking amused at the notion.

"Well, we can do that," Hyeri said confidently. "I'm sure my visions will lead us to it and between the three of you, you should be able to kill it."

Kiha gave a small laugh at that as Haru looked melancholy.

"I'm sorry," Haru said. "I can't help you."

"What? Why?" Hyeri asked. "You're a god, aren't you?"

"It doesn't work that way here," Haru replied.

There was a bitterness to his voice and once again Hyeri found herself almost catching a glimpse of the true personality that lay beneath the pretty outer layer.

"What about you?" Hyeri asked Kiha. "Are you a god too?"

"Absolutely not," Haru said harshly, sounding almost disgusted by the insinuation. "He's a demon."

"Well, can you help us destroy this Soul Eater?" Hyeri asked, not caring what he was as long as he could provide some extra muscle.

"I don't help humans," Kiha replied.

Hyeri sighed.

"Great, so it's just the two of us against some soul-sucking monster from another dimension?"

"Hey, hey, I never agreed to anything," Dongwoon piped up.

"Seriously? Even now, you're acting like this?"

"I told you before..."

"So you're fine just leaving these people like this? Like lifeless zombies?"

"No, I just..."

Hyeri wouldn't let him finish. She was sick of his constant bullshit.

"You're so selfish!" she exploded. "Can't you just put aside your own personal feelings for once and do the right thing!"

He seemed properly chastised at that, as the smug look he usually had was gone, replaced by a look of sadness in his eyes.

"I'm sorry," he said quietly and Hyeri couldn't believe he was actually apologizing.

This small bit of progress was cut short, however, by Haru's interruption.

"The Soul Eater is not important right now," he said. "What's important is closing the rifts and stopping your world from ripping apart."

"The Soul Eater should be near the rift it came from," Kiha pointed out. "It can draw more power from that rift. Find one; you'll find the other."

"Okay, so I just need to wait for a vision," Hyeri said. "That should lead me to it. In the meantime, what do we do with them? We can't just leave them here."

She gestured toward the expressionless people still sitting on the pavement.

"I'll take care of them," Haru said. "You two should get back to your job, before you get fired."

"Oh shit!" Dongwoon exclaimed. "I'm going to be late for my scene!"

"It's okay," Hyeri said, "I can pretend I collapsed outside, and you were taking care of me."

"They're going to think we're secretly dating at this rate..."

"Well, is that such a bad rumour?"

"Yes."

"It could be helpful, you know."

"Don't even joke."

She watched as Dongwoon took off running back to the studio, back to try and salvage his job.

"You two are very strange," Haru commented and Hyeri could only agree.

SHE SPENT the next week waiting patiently for a vision to hit her, but none came. She had thought one was about to once, while she was having her morning coffee, but it had turned out to be just a sneeze. She was starting to get a little bit frustrated with her bad luck. Normally she wouldn't have wanted her powers to rear their ugly head, but right now the fate of those soulless people was weighing heavily on her mind. She wanted to help them. She couldn't accept that they were just lost causes. She had to kill the Soul Eater. Even if she wasn't sure exactly how.

Dongwoon was back to his usual aloof self. But she was sure he'd help her when it came down to it. If only she could have a vision and find out exactly where this creature came from. She was sure once that happened Haru and Kiha would show up too. She hadn't seen either of them since that night on the bridge, but somehow, she knew they weren't far away from her. She wondered why they couldn't just help her. Well, she knew why Kiha wouldn't. He obviously looked down on them for being humans. But what was Haru's deal?

Someone claiming to be a god must have some pretty amazing powers, she figured. So why couldn't he use them to help her out?

It was something she often pondered those days, in between looking after Heekyung. The one upside to not having any visions was being able to fully focus on her job. She hadn't had to stop filming or run away again and Heekyung seemed more than satisfied with her abilities as an assistant. Truthfully, she enjoyed working for him. Even without being contrasted to Ms. Han's horrific behaviour, he was always so nice toward her and never demanding in his requests. Hyeri actually found herself looking forward to seeing him in the morning. Now that was something that had never happened to her before on her other jobs. She had looked after other actors before but had never found herself quite enjoying the time as she was now. She tried not to think too hard about what that meant. She had too many other things to focus on.

At the moment she was currently focused on which dress she should wear for her night out with Minki and friends. Once again, she would be heading to Hongdae for an evening of drinking, although this time she hoped there would be no subway electrocutions or run-ins with monsters.

Thankfully, there was neither on her way there and soon she was seated around a grill with Minki and three other couples, preparing to eat some delicious pork belly. The restaurant was packed full of people this time of night, so they sat squished together, the smell of grilled meat wafting all around them.

Hyeri hadn't realized when she had accepted the invitation that she would be Minki's stand-in "date" for the evening. His other friends were all in long-term relationships and he was the only woefully single one. Hyeri agreed to go only on the condition that Minki explain that they were just good friends. She refused to pretend to be his girlfriend, something that Minki wholeheartedly agreed with.

"I'd never ask you to do that," he had said. "It'd be too weird."

Definitely, Hyeri had agreed. Minki was far too much like her brother for her to see him that way. Of course, that didn't stop his friends from chiming in with their opinions.

"Oh, why don't you two just get together?" Woojin's girlfriend, Eunha, asked. "You'd make such a pretty couple."

"You probably know more about each other than we do," Woojin said, turning over the sizzling strips of pork belly on the grill with a pair of tongs.

Hyeri said nothing and instead took a long sip from her beer.

"It'd be so wrong," Minki said, shaking his head. "Like dating my sister..."

"Was there ever a time you almost did something?" Yebin asked. "Like one drunken night..."

"What about that Valentine's Day?" Youngpil piped up and Minki smacked him.

"Ooh, what happened on Valentine's Day?" Yebin asked with interest.

Hyeri was interested to hear too. She assumed Youngpil was referring to the Valentine's Day two years ago. Hyeri had gone on a date that had ended badly and wound up drinking mostly by herself until Minki had come to collect her and taken her home. She had woken up the next morning with a horrific hangover and no memory of the previous night. She knew most girls would have been concerned about that memory loss, but she knew Minki would never have done anything to her. She trusted him with her life.

"Yes, what happened on Valentine's Day?" Hyeri asked, giving him a pointed look. "Because I don't remember. I blacked out that night."

The smile disappeared from Yebin's face as she suddenly seemed more interested in helping Woojin serve up the meat.

"You didn't tell her?" Youngpil asked, clearly not able to read a room.

"Tell me what?" Hyeri asked, feeling somewhat nervous now.

What salacious tales had Minki been telling his friends? Had something really happened that night?

"It's nothing," Minki said, looking like he desperately wanted to change the subject. "You just..."

"You definitely weren't thinking of him as a brother then," Youngpil said with a laugh.

"Oh my God, Minki, did you actually…" Hyeri trailed off, not able to complete her thought.

"What? No!" Minki exclaimed. "You came on to me!"

Only Youngpil was snickering. The rest of the table were now all very interested in serving the meat.

"So did we…" Hyeri couldn't finish her sentence.

"No. Nothing happened," Minki said. "You just… kept trying to kiss me. But I refused. So you got annoyed and went to bed."

"That's not what you told me," Youngpil said, ever helpful. "You said you had to lock yourself in the bathroom 'cause she just wouldn't stop!"

He was too busy laughing to notice the death glare Minki was giving him.

"Oh my God," Hyeri muttered, feeling thoroughly embarrassed.

No wonder Minki hadn't told her anything before. It was humiliating. Imagine being so forceful that your almost-brother had to lock himself away from you.

"Shots, anyone?" Woojin offered, trying to breach the awkward situation with more alcohol.

He began pouring the soju. Hyeri gulped hers down without waiting to say cheers with the others. Then she quickly excused herself to the washroom. But on her way there she felt a strange feeling, like eyes watching her. Her hand instinctively reached up to touch the sun pendant tucked under her shirt. She didn't know why she continued to wear it. Something about its presence was just comforting. As she passed by the window, she knew what the strange feeling was. She could see just a hint of black at the window's edge, but even with just that small glimpse she knew right away who had followed her here. Swerving away from the washroom, she made her way outside. There she saw Kiha leaning against the wall, scowling at her.

"Why are you here?" she asked. "You want to join our party?"

"Hardly."

"Then why are you following me?"

"I'm waiting for you to have a vision. What's taking you so long?"

"I don't know. I don't have any control over it. Besides, why do you care? You said you wouldn't help us with the Soul Eater."

"You're right, I don't care about the Soul Eater."

"So, then... the rift. You want me to lead you to the rift it came out of. Why?"

"That's none of your business. Now just have a vision already."

His eyes changed to that golden colour once again, and he bared his fangs at her, growling slightly as he leaned in. Hyeri would not be so easily intimidated though.

"Stop that!" she said, and she smacked him on the shoulder.

Kiha seemed surprised and his fangs retracted.

"You know what, I'm sick and tired of all you men acting like assholes all the time!" Hyeri exploded. "I don't need this!"

She tried to storm off, but Kiha grabbed her arm.

"You're not afraid of me?" he asked.

"I see ghosts and monsters all the time now," Hyeri replied. "You don't scare me."

She tore her arm out of his grasp and left him, heading back inside the restaurant. If she had bothered to look back, she might have seen the small smile playing at the corners of Kiha's mouth.

She was about to resume her drinking when her phone rang. Fed up, she answered without looking at the caller ID.

"Yes? What is it?" she asked brusquely, half expecting it to be some new guy come to make her life even more difficult.

"Hyeri? It's Heekyung. Is this a bad time?"

"Oh," she said. "No, no, I'm sorry. I... I thought it was somebody else."

"I just really need your help," Heekyung went on. "How are your makeup skills? Both my stylists are suddenly sick, and I need some help tomorrow morning. It's okay if you can't do it. I just thought I would ask. You know, save production some trouble."

"Oh sure, I can do it," Hyeri proclaimed.

Truthfully, she wasn't sure her skills were up to par with a professional stylist, but there was something that just made her want to take on Heekyung's request, no matter what. She just didn't want to disappoint him. Is that really all it is? a little voice inside her asked and Hyeri willed it to go away.

"That's great," Heekyung said. "You'll have to come in a little earlier. Is that okay?"

"It's totally okay," Hyeri replied, a little too enthusiastically, and she felt her cheeks flush.

"Alright, I'll see you bright and early tomorrow morning!"

"Yes, see you then."

She didn't know why her stomach was in knots as she hung up the phone. Maybe she had drunk too much already. But once again that little voice piped up. It's not the alcohol and you know it. You're excited to see him tomorrow. She tried to distract herself with the prospect of pork belly as she headed back to her table. But it was hard when all she could think about was Heekyung's voice, soft and melodic in her ear.

THAT NIGHT she did not sleep well. She kept having strange dreams. But in the morning, she couldn't remember a single one. She just knew that they had been terrifying. All through her morning routine she couldn't shake the ominous feeling she had. She tried hard to remember something, any little thing. Then it came to her.

Just a single phrase, but one that chilled her to the bone. She remembered an eerie voice saying, "Hello, world." That was it; that was all she could recall. She didn't know why it was so frightening, but just the thought of it made her not want to remember any more. So she stopped trying to think of her dreams and instead focused on getting ready for work.

Heekyung was there to greet her when she arrived. Even barefaced he was extremely beautiful.

"I hate that you have to see me like this," he said modestly.

"Why?" Hyeri asked. "Right now, you're still prettier than me."

Heekyung laughed softly and Hyeri felt her sour mood begin to brighten a little at the sound.

"Oh, don't say that," Heekyung replied. "You're very pretty."

She knew he was just saying it to be polite, but it still made her a little bit happy just to hear those words from him.

"I almost forgot," he went on. "I have something for you."

He held out a small paper gift bag and Hyeri took it from him. She opened it up to reveal a pair of socks with a cute little Shiba Inu embroidered on top.

"Oh, thank you," Hyeri said, her cheeks feeling warm.

"I know it's not much, but I just wanted to cheer you up. And I thought about getting some jewellery, but that seemed a little... suffocating? I didn't want it to be a burden."

If Hyeri didn't know any better, she'd say he sounded a little bit flustered. But she was sure it was her imagination.

"They're really cute," she said sincerely. "Thank you, I'll put them on right away."

"Oh, you don't have to do that," Heekyung said, looking almost bashful.

Hyeri didn't know why she was feeling so strange. She'd received gifts before, some more lavish than this, from the actors she'd worked for in the past, thanking her for her services. So why did the sight of a pair of socks make her heart beat faster? She tried to remain professional on the outside while inside she felt like a schoolgirl with a silly crush.

True to her word, she took a moment to remove her shoes and then her socks (praying that there was no smell) before putting on the Shiba ones. They were so cute, she almost felt bad for putting them into her old, worn-out shoes. After that she got to work helping Heekyung with his makeup. It was fairly straightforward and less work than doing girls' makeup. Mostly it was about perfecting his already perfect features and making him look flawless. Something that wasn't hard to do given what she was working with.

"You're really good at this," Heekyung remarked as he admired his face in the mirror. "Maybe I should have hired you as my stylist instead."

"Well, I didn't have to do much," Hyeri admitted. "Most of it is you."

"You're too kind, really. I know I'm not the young rising star anymore. I'm almost forty..."

He frowned at his reflection, making lines appear on his forehead. Hyeri made a dismissive noise.

"You look better than all the twenty-somethings here," she told him.

"Is that so? Even Minki?"

"Yes."

"What about Dongwoon?"

"Of course!"

"So you really don't have a crush on him?"

"What? Absolutely not!" Hyeri said, then realized she shouldn't show her disgust too openly since she had told Heekyung that Dongwoon was a good guy not so long ago.

Still, the thought made her skin crawl. Sure, Dongwoon was handsome, he was an actor after all, but his bad attitude was such a turnoff that it soured her on his looks.

"I think you're just being nice," Heekyung remarked, still scrutinizing his face in the mirror.

"I'm not," Hyeri argued. She reached out to gently turn his face toward her as she began to touch up his eyebrows. "You're probably the most handsome guy in this whole studio."

The words left her lips before she fully realized what she was saying. But then it was out there and there was nothing she could do to take it back. The room was quiet for a moment, then Heekyung finally spoke.

"Do you really mean that?" he asked.

His earlier playfulness was gone and now he sounded serious, his eyes glancing up at Hyeri expectantly. She swallowed hard, unsure of how to respond. Should she play it off as just joking around? But that might hurt his feelings. Or should she say how she really felt? That she really did find him more handsome than any other guy there. She'd never encountered this dilemma before. She'd never found herself feeling this way about a client of hers until now.

She was sure only a second had passed, but it felt like an eternity, the air thick between them. Then something happened to break her troubled silence.

"Oh my God," Hyeri exclaimed. "Your nose..."

Heekyung looked in the mirror to see the thin line of bright red blood coming out from his nostril.

"Oh no, not again," he said with a sigh as Hyeri went to grab him some tissues.

"Here, let me see," Hyeri said, but he waved her away as he took the tissues from her and pressed them to his nose.

"It's okay," he assured her. "I'll be fine."

He tilted his head back, trying to stave off the bleeding.

"This has happened before, hasn't it?" Hyeri asked.

"Yes, for the last couple weeks. I guess I'm just working too hard. Especially at my age..."

He gave a laugh, but it sounded a little nervous to Hyeri.

"You should let production know," she said. "If they're working you this hard…"

"No, no, I don't want to bother them. It's fine, really."

"Are you sure?"

She remembered the bloody tissues in the wastebasket in his apartment. He'd been working hard for a while now.

"Yes, don't worry. I'll be okay. See, it's stopped already."

He pulled away the tissues to show his now healed nose. Hyeri bent down to inspect it herself, surprised when he flinched away from her.

"I'm glad it wasn't too serious this time," she said, "but you really should let someone know."

"No. Please, let's just keep this between us. Please, Hyeri."

She didn't know why he was pleading with her now. It had only been a suggestion, not a threat. He touched her arm gingerly, as if he wanted to grab on to her for support but was too afraid to.

"Alright," she said. "I won't say anything. But promise me you'll see a doctor at least."

"I will," he assured her. "But can you do me a favour?" He put the bloody tissues into the discarded gift bag her socks had come in. "Could you throw this away somewhere else? I don't want someone to see it in my dressing room and start rumours."

"Of course, no problem."

She took the bag from him and headed out into the hall. She planned to throw it away in the girls' washroom where no one would suspect a thing. She didn't get very far before she heard the dreaded *click-clack* of high heels coming down the hall. Hyeri felt her shoulders instinctively hunch without meaning to. She knew who it was even before they came around the corner.

"Well, look who it is," Ms. Han said. "Heekyung's new little fling."

"I'm not a fling," Hyeri replied. "He's my client."

Ms. Han raised an eyebrow.

"Oh, really?" she said. "Well, when you worked for me, I don't remember you making any personal house calls."

That was true. Mostly because Ms. Han would have never allowed a lowly commoner like Hyeri to enter her building.

"We were just going over some lines," Hyeri said.

"So it is true. You went over to his apartment."

She saw the malicious smile spread across Ms. Han's face and Hyeri mentally smacked herself for falling into that trap. She shouldn't have said anything at all.

"I must admit, he does move fast," Ms. Han went on.

"Nothing like that happened," Hyeri countered.

"Right. So you're telling me you got your job on

your merits? You? Please. You slept your way into that position."

"Excuse me? Who are you to say that to me?"

Ms. Han looked at her in disbelief, incredulous that Hyeri had dared to talk back to her.

"Who am *I*?" she asked, her voice rising. "How dare you talk to me like that! You little whore!"

There was a bright flash of light and Ms. Han let out a strangled cry as something fell from the ceiling right in front of her. Hyeri jumped back too. It was a fluorescent light, now hanging from some wires, dangling between the two of them. Its sudden fall seemed to have shocked the fight right out of Ms. Han. Or at least sent her anger in another direction. Because now she was ranting about unsafe sets and staff not keeping the building up to code. Thankfully, she chose to avoid the swinging light fixture and went off down the hall, no doubt looking for some poor crew member to yell at.

Some might have thought it a lucky coincidence. But Hyeri knew better. She knew that light had been no accident. Her assumption was correct as she walked around the corner and found Dongwoon standing there.

"I thought you hated me," she said, a sly grin on her face.

"I don't hate you; I just dislike you," Dongwoon clarified. "But her? I really hate her."

"Well, thank you anyway."

"Don't mention it. Really. Don't mention it to anyone."

"Of course," Hyeri replied. "Your secret's safe with me, Mr. Superpowers."

"Don't call me that. And you owe me one. Actually, you owe me many now."

"Ugh, can't you just be nice for once?"

"This is me being nice."

"Whatever."

And Hyeri left him to go dispose of the tissues. When she came back to the dressing room Heekyung wasn't there. Hyeri waited for him to come back, figuring he must have gone to the bathroom, but when he still hadn't returned after some time she began to worry. The crew had even come looking for him, wondering why he wasn't on set yet. Hyeri hoped he hadn't passed out somewhere. Her anxiety growing, she grabbed her phone and dialled his number.

Bzzzz.

Bzzzz.

Bzzzz.

The phone in Heekyung's pocket vibrated again and again. But he didn't answer it. Instead, he stared into the bathroom mirror, unmoving, unblinking. He didn't know why he was doing it. Just that he felt compelled to do so. He couldn't stop himself.

Bzzzz.

Bzzzz.

Bzzzz.

He knew they were calling him now. He knew they were wondering where he was. But he couldn't stop staring in the mirror. He wasn't looking at himself. He was looking at the darkness behind him. There was a shadow there, great and ominous, looming over his reflection. It filled him with all sorts of dread looking at it, but he couldn't seem to tear his eyes away.

Please, I have to go.

Please, let me go.

Please.

Let!

Me!

Go!

And just like that he felt his body able to finally move again. He sucked in a huge breath of air as relief washed over him. Then his body became wracked by coughs. He leaned over the sink and coughed up something. He felt a sense of terror sweep over him as he spat out a mouthful of a thick, black gooey substance. He hastily rinsed out his mouth; then he all but ran out of the bathroom. He was in such a rush to leave he didn't notice the large crack now at the top of the mirror, identical to the one in his own home.

Five

Filming had been going well for most of the day. It wasn't until later in the evening that Heekyung began to falter. Hyeri watched as the normally composed and focused actor suddenly needed more takes than usual to complete his scenes. She could see Ms. Han getting annoyed with him, the actress's short fuse even shorter after the incident with the light that morning.

"I'm sorry, can we stop for a moment?" Heekyung finally asked. "I have a migraine and I think I need to take some medicine for it before we continue."

"Yes, of course," the director said. "We'll break for fifteen and then get back to it."

He had more than enough patience for Heekyung, who had always been nice and professional. Ms. Han on the other hand, had zero patience, as was to be expected. As Heekyung headed back to his dressing room, she followed him out into the hall. Hyeri followed the two as well, feeling protective over her new client.

"You know," Ms. Han said to him, "maybe you should spend more time rehearsing your lines instead of hooking up with assistants."

"That's not what happened, and you know it," Heekyung replied wearily.

"Right. Of course not. She's a bit young for you anyway, don't you think?"

"Just drop it."

Hyeri was about to intervene as it seemed Ms. Han wasn't ready to let it go, but a commotion down the end of the hall interrupted her.

"Junyoung, where are you going?" someone yelled. "Why won't you listen to me? Junyoung!"

A dishevelled young man rounded the corner. Hyeri noticed the blank look in his eyes first. He was definitely a victim of the Soul Eater. Then she noticed what he was holding in his hand.

A knife.

Heekyung and Ms. Han must have seen it too. The two of them stood there frozen, staring at the man.

"What do you want? Let's just talk," Heekyung said calmly, trying to defuse the situation.

The man didn't reply, just as Hyeri knew he wouldn't. Slowly, she positioned herself in front of Heekyung and Ms. Han. She didn't know what she was going to do, but she just knew she had to protect

Heekyung. Somehow, she would find a way. Suddenly the man's expression changed as he fixated on Hyeri.

"Light," he muttered. "Light..."

He began to walk forward, and the trio backed up in response. His friend rounded the corner now, but upon seeing the knife simply ran the other way.

The crazed man was now coming faster at them, brandishing the knife as he cried out, "Liiiiight." Hyeri was about to tell the others to run away, when to her horror Ms. Han did the unthinkable. Hyeri watched, helpless, as Ms. Han grabbed Heekyung and pushed him in front of her and Hyeri before making a break for it. The world went gray at that moment. Hyeri saw the crazed man raise the knife, ready to strike. She braced herself for the end result, fully expecting to see Heekyung get stabbed right before her eyes without anything she could do to stop it.

But that's not what happened. Instead of bringing the knife down, the man abruptly stopped, his arm held in midair. And as he looked at Heekyung fully, he began to shrink back, cowering in fear. Hyeri didn't know what was happening. Why was the man suddenly so afraid of Heekyung? She didn't have time to wonder though as at that moment Dongwoon stepped out into the hall. As soon as he appeared the crazed man's demeanour changed. He stopped cowering and with a cry of "Light!" he flew at Dongwoon, knife out.

Dongwoon quickly held up his hands, and the man flew backward without being touched. It wasn't enough to stop him though, and he was still holding that knife. The man stood up to attack again and this time Dongwoon looked up at the ceiling. Just like before, one of the light fixtures came crashing down. Only this time it connected with its target. Hyeri watched as bolts of blue electricity cascaded through the light and into the crazed man. He shook and convulsed as he was electrocuted and then he lay still on the ground. Hyeri turned away as she saw a small line of blood seep out of the man's mouth. She knew at that moment that he was dead. She looked over at Dongwoon. He was staring in shock, his eyes wide and horrified.

By now people were coming out into the hall, drawn by the noise. Hyeri saw Minki and went over to him.

"Don't look," she told him.

"What... Oh my God. What happened?"

"He... he just came at me," Dongwoon was mumbling. "He had a knife... I don't..."

"He was crazy or something," Heekyung said. "He tried to stab Dongwoon. We're lucky that light fell on him."

Lucky. Hyeri knew it hadn't been luck. She knew the real cause of that man's death was Dongwoon.

FILMING WAS HALTED AFTER THAT, and the police were called. They questioned Hyeri and the others, asking if anyone knew a motive for the attack, but no one could think of one, not even his friend. The preliminary ruling was that his death had been an accident, caused by the falling light and the police would only be investigating for negligence in the building standards. They left with the warning that Hyeri and the others may be called in for more questioning.

"That was intense," Minki exclaimed after the police had left with the deceased man's friend.

"Definitely," Heekyung agreed.

Dongwoon said nothing. He still looked quite shell-shocked over the whole thing.

"Are you okay?" Hyeri asked him.

"Yeah," he mumbled unconvincingly.

He didn't look at her. Instead, he had a thousand-yard stare, one that closely resembled that of the Soul Eater's victims. Hyeri was worried for him.

"You know what we need right now?" Heekyung said. "A stiff drink. Let's get out of here and go somewhere else. I'm buying."

"Yeah, that sounds like a plan," Minki said somberly and Hyeri and Dongwoon agreed.

Of course, they did not invite Ms. Han even though she had been there for part of the ordeal. When everyone else had been at a loss for a motive, she had mentioned that the man seemed interested in Hyeri, but Heekyung had come to Hyeri's defence, reiterating that the man was just crazy. Neither he nor Hyeri brought up Ms. Han's cowardly move of trying to sacrifice Heekyung so she could escape, even though

Hyeri had the sneaking suspicion that it was more than just self-preservation that had motivated the actress to do that.

The four of them decided on a bar not too far from the studio. It was an old-fashioned place, playing some trot music over tinny speakers while an elderly couple tended to the only table they had, a group of balding, middle-aged businessmen. It seemed the perfect place to grab a quiet corner table and drink until you forgot. Which was what they did. Heekyung ordered a bottle of soju for each of them, and they downed shot after shot like there was no tomorrow. And in no time at all, the four of them were all very drunk.

"So then I was scrolling his social media," Hyeri went on, halfway through her embarrassing tale, "and I accidentally liked a picture of him from four years ago!"

Minki was giggling as Heekyung gasped.

"Noooo," Heekyung exclaimed. "Really?"

"Yes, and it was a picture of him on the beach, shirtless too," Hyeri said.

Heekyung and Minki were both cracking up at her misfortune. Dongwoon, however, seemed unmoved.

"I still can't believe you eventually confessed to him," Minki said, pouring them all another shot. "That was very bold of you."

"You did?" Heekyung asked, sounding intrigued. "What did you say?"

"Oh, I don't want to bore you with the details," Hyeri replied.

"Tell him how you did it," Minki went on, goading his friend.

"I saw him out on a schedule with his client," Hyeri went on, "and I had this letter I had prepared. So I just gave it to him quickly and then ran away!"

"You literally ran!" Minki laughed.

"Oh my," Heekyung commented. "I can't imagine confessing to a co-worker in a letter..."

"Well, how would you do it then?" Hyeri asked.

Heekyung looked her in the eyes and despite her drunkenness she could see the sincerity in them.

"I would tell them straight to their face," he replied and Hyeri didn't know how to respond.

She felt her chest tightening, like her heart was being squeezed, and she knew if Heekyung kept looking at her like that she was going to start blushing.

"I could never ask out someone I worked with," Minki piped up. "It would be too awkward."

Heekyung looked away at that and it was as if a spell was broken and Hyeri was free to breathe again.

"Yes, well, it was extremely awkward when I had to see him again at the company afterward," Hyeri said. "I'd never confess again unless I knew for sure that the other person felt the same way."

"What about you?" Minki asked, nudging Dongwoon. "Do you have any similar stories?"

"What? Oh, no, not really," Dongwoon replied solemnly.

"Are you okay?" Minki asked him. "You've been so quiet."

"I just... keep seeing it in my head," Dongwoon replied. "That man..."

Hyeri felt the mood of the table shift. They had managed to steer clear of sombre topics for some time now, but inevitably the conversation had come back to the incident.

"It was bad," Minki agreed. "But there wasn't anything you could do. He was attacking you guys."

"It was lucky that light fell when it did," Heekyung added. "Or one of us could have been stabbed."

Hyeri saw Dongwoon's face change at that. He looked sickened.

"I shouldn't have done it," he muttered.

"What? Pushed him?" Heekyung asked. "Don't worry about that. That push didn't kill him."

"I shouldn't have used my—"

Hyeri was about to shush him and his drunken rambling, but she was beaten to it.

"Hyeri! Imagine seeing you here!"

All eyes turned toward the voice, Dongwoon's confession lost in the shift in attention. It was Haru, once again popping up unexpectedly. The cute silver-haired god made his way over to the table and put his hand on Hyeri's shoulder, his grip just a little too hard for her liking.

"Hi," he said introducing himself to Heekyung and Minki. "I'm Hyeri's cousin, Haru."

The two greeted him as Haru pulled over an empty chair and situated himself between Hyeri and Dongwoon.

"What are you doing here?" Hyeri asked.

"I was just in the area and felt like a drink," Haru replied. "Never thought I'd see you in a place like this."

"Yeah, well, we had a rough day at work," Hyeri said.

"Well what better way to get over it than by drinking yourselves into oblivion," Haru remarked. "Shall we have another bottle?"

Hyeri was not excited for more alcohol, but felt she couldn't say no. She especially didn't want to leave with Heekyung still there, though she tried hard to ignore the reason why. Then she felt it. That dull ache inside her head. A vision? Finally, after all this time? She was relieved to be finally receiving one, but at the same time she didn't want to experience it in front of Heekyung and Minki. She didn't know what she would see or what her reaction would be to it. So she excused herself to the restroom.

As she stood in front of the bathroom mirror, she waited for the vision to hit, but nothing came. She started to wonder if maybe the headache was just from all the soju she had drunk. With a sigh, Hyeri walked into one of the stalls. If she was in the bathroom already, she might as well use her time wisely. She noticed all too late the stall was out of toilet paper. And she had left her purse at the table. Shit.

Before she could think of a creative alternative, she

noticed the feet in the stall next to hers. Good, she might just be saved after all.

"Um, excuse me," Hyeri started, knocking lightly on the stall wall, "can I borrow some paper? There's none in here."

There was silence from the next stall, although she saw the girl's leg twitch slightly at the sound of her voice.

"I'm sorry to bother you," Hyeri tried again, "but could you please lend me some toilet paper?"

Still nothing from the other girl. And then, just as Hyeri was about to plead for a third time, a voice rasped out, "Red or blue paper?"

Hyeri felt her stomach drop at those words. There was an urban legend when she had been in school, about a ghost who haunted the bathrooms there. If you ran out of paper, the ghost would pretend to be another classmate, ready to help. But they would ask you a strange question, red or blue paper. If you chose red, the ghost was said to cut your throat. If you chose blue, the spirit would strangle you instead. Of course, this "spirit" was just students playing a prank on their classmates and the only consequence of hearing that question was your friends having a laugh at your expense. But these days Hyeri wasn't sure what to expect. She tried hard to remember the correct answer to the question. What was it that would save her neck?

"Neither!" Hyeri finally called out, remembering that if you rejected either option, the spirit was said to leave you alone.

There was a dismissive noise from the other stall.

"Tsk, you're no fun," the voice said and then a roll of toilet paper was kicked into her stall.

Hyeri used it quickly then rushed out, ready to confront the practical joker. But when she approached the other stall, it was empty. She felt the hairs on the back of her neck stand up as she realized she hadn't actually heard the stall door or the door to the bathroom open before seeing the feet in the stall next to hers. And now there was no one in the bathroom at all.

So it really had been a ghost. Well, she wasn't going to waste any time pondering if it was just one messing with her or the real urban legend, so she hightailed it out of the bathroom. But just as she was opening the door she was suddenly struck with a vision.

It was Dongwoon. And he was surrounded by soulless people. That was the only image she got before the world returned to normal. She was so distracted by it she didn't notice Haru waiting for her right outside the bathroom.

"Something's wrong with your friend," Haru said and Hyeri jumped.

"Jeez, you startled me," she exclaimed. "Can you stop doing that, just popping up out of nowhere? And yeah, Dongwoon is pretty freaked out by the whole incident that happened at the studio today. We were attacked by a victim of the Soul Eater."

"I don't mean him. I mean the other one. Heekyung,

was it? There's something strange about him, but I'm not sure what it is."

"Maybe he has a power, like me and Dongwoon," Hyeri suggested.

"Maybe," was all Haru replied.

The thought was an attractive one to Hyeri. If Heekyung had a power like them, then she wouldn't have to be so secretive around him. And she was sure he'd be more helpful than Dongwoon. Speaking of...

"Oh, I had a vision finally," Hyeri said, and she saw that Haru looked far more interested in this than talk of Heekyung. "But it was just about Dongwoon. I need to tell him to be more careful."

"Oh, he already left."

"What!"

"He said he was taking a taxi home."

"I need to find him!"

Hyeri ran out of the bar and scanned the street around her. Why was this always happening? Why were her visions always so late? Couldn't they come like a week in advance? That would make her life so much easier. She looked around frantically for any sign of Dongwoon. Then she heard something coming from the alleyway. As she rounded the corner, she saw three soulless people surrounding Dongwoon, all of them mumbling about "light."

"Go away," Dongwoon told them as he feebly pushed them back. "Stay away from me!"

Hyeri was confused. Why wasn't he using his powers? Why was he fighting back so weakly?

"Dongwoon!" she called out as she ran toward him.

She tried to pull one of the people off him, but it was no use. They were all completely fixated on Dongwoon. One of the men suddenly bit into Dongwoon's arm and he cried out in pain. So they really were like zombies now, were they? Hyeri knew she had to do something quick. But what? She just had visions and saw ghosts. She was a defensive player at best.

"Use your power!" Hyeri told Dongwoon.

"I can't," he said. "I won't. I won't kill anyone else."

He cried out again as another person latched on to his other arm, sinking in their teeth like an aggressive dog. Hyeri tried to pull the soulless person off, but they only bit down harder. As she touched the biting woman she was rewarded with a vision. It wasn't of much use to her though. Just an image of moulting black feathers and sharp teeth. She guessed it was the Soul Eater's true form.

"You can do it," Hyeri told Dongwoon. "I know you can do it without killing them."

"I can't..."

"Just trust me! I'll guide you."

Hyeri took his hand in hers and focused all her energy on subduing the people and not killing them. There was a flash of bright white light and Hyeri felt a shock, like an electric current running through her. She closed her eyes tightly, wishing, "Please don't kill them."

When she opened her eyes, the zombie people were all on the ground, lying motionless.

"Are they dead?" Dongwoon asked, looking distraught.

Hyeri put her hand in front of one of the men's noses. She sighed in relief as she felt a puff of air against her fingers.

"They're alive," she said. "Just unconscious, it looks like."

Dongwoon made a strangled noise that almost sounded like a sob.

"Thank God," he replied, breathily.

"Come on," Hyeri said. "Let's get out of here before they wake up." She looked at Dongwoon's bleeding arms. "We should get that looked at too."

"I'm fine," he told her.

"So I guess we're even now. Since I saved you this time."

"I saved you twice. Three, if you count that demon guy grabbing you."

"Does it really matter how many times?"

"Yes."

"Okay, well I'll wake them up and then I can save you again."

"You're not funny."

"Funnier than you, at least."

Once again, the two of them were too busy arguing to notice a shadowy figure standing on the rooftop behind them. Kiha sheathed his sword as he watched

Hyeri and Dongwoon go. He wouldn't need to use it tonight at least.

<hr>

As Heekyung waited for Minki to return from the washroom, he found himself doodling absent-mindedly on a napkin. He hated being alone these days. Sometimes he found that the time passed so quickly when he was alone without him even noticing at all. It was unnerving to say the least. He hoped the others would return soon. He at least wanted to say goodbye to Hyeri before he left.

Hyeri.

Just the thought of her made him smile. There was just something about her that made him feel happier when she was around. She was like a breath of fresh air amidst all the stuffy company people he dealt with on a regular basis.

"Ready to go?" Minki asked as he came back to the table and Heekyung stuffed the napkin he'd been drawing on into his pocket. "I think Hyeri just went to say goodbye to Dongwoon."

Ah yes, Dongwoon. Heekyung still wasn't entirely convinced that Hyeri didn't have a crush on him. The two always seemed to be running off together or having private conversations. He felt a twinge of sadness as he thought about it. Dongwoon was probably closer to Hyeri's age. He was sure Dongwoon had more in common with her than he did. And now they were outside, alone together. Maybe they were making out already, the bastard.

No, don't think like that. Heekyung scolded his brain and its wayward thoughts. Dongwoon was really traumatized after what happened today. Hyeri was probably just making sure he was okay.

"Poor Dongwoon," Heekyung commented. "He was really shaken up by today."

"Yeah, it must have been so awful," Minki agreed. "I only saw the aftermath, but that was enough. I know I'm going to have nightmares about that guy. Just seeing his face like that..."

Heekyung couldn't help it as he began to laugh. He didn't know why he did. There was nothing funny about what Minki had said. There was definitely nothing funny about what had happened today. But when he thought about the dead man all he felt was a sense of amusement. What the hell was wrong with him?

"Sorry," he said to Minki. "It's a stress reaction. I'm not really feeling like myself either."

He could see Minki looking at him strangely. He was about to try and explain further when he felt something wet on his lip.

"Your nose is bleeding," Minki pointed out.

Heekyung covered his nose with his hand and quickly excused himself to the washroom. Not again. Why was this always happening to him? He tilted his head back as he stood in front of the bathroom mirror, waiting for the bleeding to stop. Thankfully, it did after a minute. He went to grab some paper to wipe away the rest of the blood, but the machine was empty. Then he remembered the napkin in his pocket. He took it out and gasped in horror at what he saw. The doodle he had been working on earlier, it wasn't just a harmless little cartoon as he had imagined. It was a very detailed drawing of the dead man from earlier today. And that wasn't all. Around the edges he had written "ha ha ha," as if laughing at the man's death. He didn't remember doing it at all. But it was clearly his writing. With a cry of disgust, Heekyung threw the drawing into the trash bin. He wiped at his nose with his hand and quickly rinsed it off in the sink. Then he rushed back out to Minki and the others.

KIHA WATCHED them all leave from his rooftop position, feeling rather bored and somewhat annoyed. He didn't look up as he heard the door to the roof open, already knowing it was Haru coming to see him.

"I know where the Soul Eater is," Kiha said. "You know, it would be so much easier just to kill it myself."

"They have to learn to work together," Haru replied, "if they have any chance of saving this world."

"I don't care about this world..."

Haru stood beside him now, looking out at the city.

"There's nothing that can bring *her* back, if that's what you're thinking," he said.

"And how would you know? If I can find the third person..."

"What are you talking about?"

"I already have her eyes and hands. Now I just need to find her heart."

"Her heart? I thought she gave that away a long time ago," Haru said with a bitter chuckle.

"There are pieces of her still in this world. If I can find them, I can find a way to bring her back. Those two humans, they're the key. They'll lead me to her heart."

"If you say so..."

Kiha knew Haru didn't believe him, but he didn't care. Just as he didn't care about saving this pitiful world. All he cared about these days was bringing back his beloved.

He looked down at his hand. Clutched in it was a necklace with a silver pendant. It was a moon, matching the sun that Hyeri now had. Kiha clasped it tightly in his hand, more determined than ever.

Six

arkness. All-encompassing, black darkness. That was all she could see. Then, people screaming in fear and pain. Laughter, gleeful and malicious. Like that of someone who truly revelled in doing wicked things.

Terror.

Panic.

Chaos.

Darkness.

"Hello, world."

Hyeri awoke with a start. Her heart was pounding in her chest, her body covered in a cold sweat. She knew she had been dreaming, but just like every other night, she couldn't remember about what. All she knew was the feeling of sheer terror she had felt just before waking up. It frightened her so much. Even the bright sunshine peeking through her curtains was no comfort as she thought about that feeling. She wished she could remember more, but at the same time she didn't want to. What if her brain was trying to protect her by not allowing her to recall?

She looked at her clock. It was late; she should be up right now. She had the day off, but that didn't mean she wanted to spend it in bed. She had plans to go to the market today. Only now she didn't feel like going alone. She felt sufficiently spooked by her vague but terrifying nightmare and needed some moral support.

She tried Minki first, but he was busy. She thought of her other friends but realized that none of them would even be able to relate to her studio job, let alone the weird things going on lately. She tried Dongwoon second, but he didn't answer. Of course. He probably saw the caller ID and was refusing to pick up. She didn't know why she had even bothered. Call it a momentary lapse in judgment.

There was just one person left. Heekyung. But would he want to hang out with her outside of work? It was highly unorthodox. An assistant wasn't supposed to be making personal calls to their client, at least not one this new. But then again, most actors and their assistants didn't almost get stabbed together. A shared experience like that, horrible as it was, had a way of bringing people together. And if he really did have a power...

Hyeri made up her mind. She was doing it, job be damned! To her surprise Heekyung seemed more than happy to take her up on her offer.

"It'll be nice to get away from the show for once," he said. "I could use a proper day off."

And so that was how Hyeri found herself waiting at the market's entrance, nervously twisting the straps of her bag as she waited for Heekyung to arrive. She didn't know why she was so nervous. She saw him nearly every day; she should be used to it by now. But that was always at work, or in the context of work at least. This was pure leisure. Feeling fidgety, she took out her compact and began checking over her face, making sure there were no imperfections. She knew she shouldn't care so much. There was no way Heekyung would even see a plain girl like her that way. Not when he was surrounded by beautiful actresses and entertainers day in and day out.

"You look great!" she heard a familiar voice say.

Startled, Hyeri snapped the compact shut and looked up to see Heekyung standing in front of her. He was slightly more dressed up than he had been at his apartment, although he was still in all black. Thankfully, he was not wearing bright red slippers this time.

"I mean, you don't have to fix anything," Heekyung went on. "Your makeup, I mean. It looks fine. Oh, not fine. Good. It looks good. Great!"

He seemed a bit flustered, and it made Hyeri's heart ache, thinking of the possibility of him liking her. But no, she couldn't go there. She had to remain professional.

"Thank you," she said. "Shall we go in?"

"Sure. Anything in particular you're looking for today?"

"To be honest, I mostly just come for the street food," Hyeri said and Heekyung laughed.

"That's the best part of the market, isn't it?" he replied.

"Oh, I also have a watch I wanted to repair. I know there's a shop around here that does it."

She pulled the watch out of her bag to show him. She was sure he was used to much nicer things, but this watch meant a lot to her. It was a present from her parents when she graduated from university. She felt like it was the last time they were proud of her, back when she had accomplished something, before she had squandered all her potential taking care of actors instead of "making something of herself." Of course, she hoped that would all change once she finished her script. The watch served as a reminder to keep striving to do better, to make her parents proud once more.

"It's nice," Heekyung commented. "A gift from an ex-boyfriend?"

"No, my parents."

"Ah."

Why was he concerned where it came from? No, Hyeri couldn't go down that line of thinking. It led to dangerous places. She was treading a thin line as it was.

They browsed the market shops together, tasting various delicious things along the way. There were the usual fishcakes and chicken skewers, along with deep-fried meats and vegetables and of course, *tteokbokki*. As much as she enjoyed it, Hyeri stayed away from the *tteokbokki* this time, instead opting for something a little less messy, like *bungeo ppang,* a goldfish-shaped bread filled with bean paste. Her personal favourite was the custard-filled ones, but she supposed the bean paste was just as good.

Hyeri was surprised how comfortable it was, walking around with Heekyung. Despite her initial nervousness she found that he was easy to talk to and there was never an awkward silence. Any silence there was just seemed like a natural part of the ebb and flow of the conversation. It was like they'd known each other much longer than they actually had. As if they were... destined to be together.

Stop it, stop. Stop thinking that way, Hyeri told herself. She willed the thoughts from her head. It was then that she noticed some people starting to look at them, some even pointing. For a moment she felt self-conscious, feeling that there must have been something wrong with her. Then she realized that wasn't the case. The people were focused on Heekyung. They must have recognized him. She overheard two older ladies talking to each other.

"That's him," one said. "That actor from TV."

"Are you sure?" the other asked. "What's he doing here?"

"Maybe they're going to film something."

"He sure is handsome..."

"But he doesn't dress like a celebrity at all. Those clothes don't fit right."

Hyeri made her way over to where Heekyung was looking at some mung bean pancakes.

"People are starting to recognize you," she told him quietly.

"Oh, really?"

He didn't seem all that concerned. Hyeri could still hear the older ladies talking. They weren't doing much to conceal their conversation.

"Who's that with him?"

"His girlfriend?"

"No way. Her?"

"Yeah, I doubt it…"

Hyeri bristled. Didn't those ladies know how loud they were being?

"You know, people might start rumours," Hyeri told Heekyung, "seeing the two of us…"

He looked at her then and she felt her heart skip a beat, staring into those beautiful eyes.

"Let them," he said. "I wouldn't mind it."

Then he did something that surprised her. He took her hand in his and led her away from the gossiping ladies and over to the next market stall. If Hyeri's heart had skipped a beat before, now it just about stopped. She suddenly felt hot all over and just a little bit lightheaded. Was this how it felt to have a heart attack? She didn't think it was possible for just one little touch to have such an effect on her. Why was she feeling this way now? He'd held her hand before when he was making sure she was okay. But it felt different somehow. More poignant now.

"Come on," Heekyung said, seemingly unaffected by her hand intertwined with his. "Let's go find the watch shop."

He led her through the crowded market, never once taking his hand away, even though they were now out of sight of the older ladies. Was it just a ploy to mess with people's heads? Or was there something more at play? Hyeri felt like she shouldn't even dare dream that. He was just being funny, trying to make people gossip even harder, that was all. She really shouldn't read more into it; she knew that. But still, it was nice walking around hand in hand like this. She could almost imagine it was a date. And it had been so long since she'd been on one of those.

"Is this it?" Heekyung asked as they neared a small shop at the end of the market.

Hyeri nodded and sadly Heekyung let go of her hand.

"I'll just be a moment," she said. "It's pretty boring in there so why don't you check out the food on this side and I'll meet you."

The shop was very small, and she worried about being in such a tight space with him with the way she was feeling at the moment. She was sure her face was going to betray her and reveal her true feelings if he got too close. Nope, better that he stay outside for now. Heekyung seemed none the wiser to her inner struggle as he headed off to one of the food stalls, mulling over the different options. It only took Hyeri a minute to explain to the watch repairman the problem and drop off her watch, but when she exited the shop, she couldn't see Heekyung anywhere. What she did see, however, was a familiar face, scowling at her as he shoved his way roughly through the crowd. It was Kiha. And he looked none too pleased, as usual.

"Why haven't you seen anything yet?" he asked her.

"Nice to see you too," she replied sarcastically. "I don't know, maybe my power's broken."

"You should have had a vision by now. If you were actually worthy of that power."

"Hey, I'm plenty worthy. And I have been having visions. At least, I think so. I keep having these weird dreams at night but... I can't remember them."

"You're completely useless."

"Look, I'm trying, okay?"

"Well try harder!"

He grabbed her by the shoulders, emphasizing his point, by leaning in and flashing his fangs.

"Hey! Let go of her!"

It was Heekyung. He had returned, holding two ice cream cones. Hyeri had never seen him look so serious before, his usually warm brown eyes now dark and stormy.

"It's okay," Hyeri said. "He was just leaving."

As Kiha turned to face Heekyung his look of anger turned to one of puzzlement. He sniffed at the air, moving toward Heekyung in a slightly predatory manner. Hyeri suddenly felt herself feeling protective.

She didn't want a fight to break out between the two of them as she was sure Heekyung would lose, powers or not. Kiha had a sword after all.

"Actually, we'll be leaving instead," Hyeri said. "Goodbye now!"

She pulled Heekyung away through the crowd, sure that Kiha wouldn't follow. He had made his point and would no doubt disappear now like he and Haru usually did. She wished they could be a teensy bit more helpful. At least in Haru's case it seemed like there was something possibly preventing him from helping them, whatever that was. But Kiha just seemed stubborn.

"Who was that guy?" Heekyung asked. "A cosplayer or something?"

"Sort of," Hyeri replied. "He belongs to this historical club, and they get a little too into it sometimes."

"Was that a sword on his back?"

"Just a prop. He's really interested in all that old stuff."

"I see. So how do you two know each other?"

"Oh, um... I was... also in the club. A long time ago." Hyeri was a bit surprised how easily the lie came to her. "He's just always whining about me coming back..."

"Well, I don't blame him. It must have been a real loss for their club."

Hyeri could have sworn Heekyung's cheeks were a little pinkish as he said it, but maybe it was just the stress of almost getting into a fight.

"Oh here, I got this for you," Heekyung said, and he handed Hyeri one of the ice cream cones.

"Oh, thank you!" Hyeri chirped.

Heekyung was about to reply when instead he was suddenly afflicted by a series of coughs. He tried to get it under control as his lungs spasmed and Hyeri became concerned.

"I'll get you some water!" she said hurriedly, and she disappeared through the crowd, running off to the nearest food stall.

***

KIHA WRINKLED his nose in disgust as he made his way out of the market. He hated the smell of the food here, so greasy and full of needless oil. He missed his homeworld. But more than that, he missed *her*. Her laugh, her smile, her sparkling eyes. There were pieces of her power left in this world, but of course it didn't compare to the real thing.

Those humans. Those filthy, lowly, undeserving humans. They were not fit to have her power inside of them.

"I don't know," a voice from beside him said. "I think you don't give them enough credit."

It was Haru. Of course, who else would dare speak to him in this awful forsaken land but the annoying god.

"That one with the visions is useless," Kiha said. "She hasn't seen anything about the rifts or the Soul Eater.

The only vision she's had was to save the other useless human."

"Just give them time. They'll learn how to handle their powers more effectively."

"I don't want them to learn. They need to give them back."

Haru let out a big sigh.

"You're still on about that?" he asked wearily.

"Why are you here anyway?" Kiha asked, annoyed.

"That friend of Hyeri's, the one with the long hair, there's something strange about him..."

"Yes, he smells different from the others. But I'm not sure what it is."

"Me neither. But I thought I'd keep an eye on him when he's with Hyeri. And by the way..." Haru moved in closer, his eyes changing from dark brown to a vibrant blue. "I saw how you treated Hyeri back there. If you hurt the humans, I'll have to step in. And I don't think you want that."

He stared at Kiha menacingly, daring him to talk back, his usually cute and cheerful face now deadly serious. Kiha was always in awe of how drastically different the change was. If he wasn't a god, Haru would have made a fierce demon.

Kiha didn't respond to Haru's threat and instead just stared back, his fangs elongating just slightly. He would never bow down to this god. Not once.

After a moment of staring each other down, Haru patted him on the shoulder patronizingly and went to leave. Kiha looked back at the market, bustling with humans. Why was Haru so keen on saving this world anyway?

As Hyeri made her way back to Heekyung she suddenly felt odd. It was as if the air had gotten colder and crisper even though it was a warm spring afternoon. Despite the crowd of people Hyeri felt very alone, as an eerie atmosphere descended upon the market. She knew this feeling all too well. There was definitely a ghost nearby. It didn't take her long to locate them. There, amidst the crowd of healthy, normal human beings was a pale, bloodied girl. Hyeri felt her stomach turn as she realized the girl was missing an eye, a dark, bloody socket all that remained. The girl reached out her arm, beckoning to Hyeri, as she mouthed the word, "Help." Then she disappeared in a flash. Hyeri was startled as the ghost vanished so quickly. She began frantically looking around, beside and behind her, expecting the girl to pop up next to her like they did in horror movies. But she was alone. At least in terms of otherworldly beings. There were definitely enough warm-bodied people around.

Remembering her task, Hyeri quickly made her way back to Heekyung and gave him the bottle of water. Then she led him over to the park at the end of the market and had him sit down on one of the benches.

"Thank you," Heekyung said, his breathing now

under control.

"Let's just sit here and rest for a bit," Hyeri offered.

Heekyung looked like he might protest, but another bout of coughing stopped him. Instead, he drank more water and dutifully sat on the bench next to Hyeri.

"I'm sorry," he said.

"What? Don't be. You're working so hard these days; you're pushing your body to its limits."

"No, not about that. I'm sorry I never stood up for you when you were working for Ms. Han. It wasn't right the way she treated you. But I didn't want to make a scene, so I said nothing. I'm so sorry. I won't be like that anymore."

"It's no problem," Hyeri said. "But you know, if she finds out about today, she'll have even more reason to come after the both of us. You know she accused me of sleeping with you?"

"That's rich, coming from her. I'll let you in on a little secret. She's been jealous of anyone close to me after I turned her down."

"What? She asked you out?"

"Not asked out. She fully came on to me in my dressing room. I was so flustered I think I was a little too rude in turning her down. She's hated me ever since."

"That's horrible."

"Anyway, once again I'm so sorry," Heekyung said.

Hyeri didn't hear the rest of what he said. A woman standing nearby had caught her attention instead. The woman was just staring at the pair of them, mumbling something. As Hyeri focused on her she realized that the woman was quietly murmuring, "Light, light." Heekyung hadn't noticed her yet and was continuing on with his apology. Hyeri was nervous for a moment until she remembered what had happened the last time. How the man with the knife had cowered in front of Heekyung. The actor seemed to be a natural repellant to victims of the Soul Eater. Hyeri was sure that as long as Heekyung was around her the soulless woman wouldn't come any closer. She wondered what kind of power he might have. And how would she ever broach the subject? "Hey, did you ever get randomly electrocuted and develop strange superpowers?" He'd think she was crazy for sure.

"Are you okay?" Heekyung asked. "You seem distracted."

"Yeah, I'm fine. I'm..."

Hyeri trailed off as a sudden idea struck her. When she touched certain objects or people, she was granted visions. When she helped Dongwoon escape the zombie people she had seen flashes of the Soul Eater. Maybe if she really held on to one of them, she would be able to see more.

"Will you excuse me for a second?" she said. "I think that's a friend of my mother's over there. She looks a little lost, so I'll just go and see if she needs some help."

She left Heekyung on the bench holding their ice creams and headed over to where the woman was standing.

"Mrs. Oh, so nice to see you," Hyeri said as she walked around to the other side, leading the woman away from Heekyung.

She knew it was dangerous to face the woman alone, but she didn't want Heekyung to get involved if things got out of hand. If he didn't have a power, she'd only be putting him in danger by mixing him up in all of this. As Hyeri rounded the corner, out of Heekyung's sight, she sprung upon the woman following her, taking both the woman's hands in hers.

And just as she had predicted, she was gifted with a vision for her efforts. She saw a horrible black, feathery creature with a large, distended mouth full of rotten teeth. It was on a mountaintop, overlooking the city. She saw an old temple and a stone marker. She knew where this was. It was Keundolsan National Park!

Hyeri let go of the woman's hands, excited that she'd finally had a proper vision. That excitement didn't last, however, as the woman's expressionless face turned angry, now that she was so close to Hyeri. The woman grabbed her arm. Hyeri tried to yank it away, but the woman seemed unusually strong.

"Light," the woman said fiercely. "Light!"

She made to bite Hyeri, but then her arm was suddenly lifted and Hyeri was pulled away. Her saviour pulled her into the alleyway, away from the woman's grasp and out of her sight. Hyeri knew the zombie woman wouldn't follow them. Most likely she had gone back to her previous state and was no doubt already wandering around aimlessly. Hyeri looked up to see who had saved her. She was surprised to see Kiha staring back at her.

"So you finally had a vision, did you? Congratulations," he said mockingly. "Did you see anything worthwhile this time?"

"Yes, actually. I saw where the Soul Eater is."

"And?"

"Why should I tell you? It's not like you're going to help us anyway."

"Did you see anything about the rifts?"

"No, just the Soul Eater."

Kiha let out an exasperated sigh.

"Why do I even bother," he muttered.

"Look, I'm not just some tool for you to use. I'm a living, breathing person, okay? Besides, you haven't told me what you want with the rifts. You're a demon, aren't you? How do I know you don't want to end the world or something?"

"I don't care about your world."

"Then what is so important about the rifts? Tell me."

Kiha looked away.

"You wouldn't understand," he muttered and Hyeri scoffed.

"Fine, keep your damn secrets," she said. "But don't bother me again. I can take care of myself."

She went to leave, but Kiha stopped her. He lifted the chain of the sun pendant around her neck.

"If you're going to wear it, you should be more

fitting of it. You should be more careful around the Soul Eater's victims. They might seem harmless, but they can do a lot of damage if left alone."

He looked her in the eyes and for the first time Hyeri felt she saw the true Kiha behind the gruff exterior. He wasn't being condescending or mocking now. He was sincerely telling her to be more careful. She felt her mood soften a little at that. But she was still annoyed at him for being so secretive.

"I'll keep that in mind," she said curtly as she pulled away from him.

Then she went back to see Heekyung. If she had turned around, she might have noticed a look of longing in Kiha's eyes as he watched her go. It was only for a moment, before he disappeared into the shadows of the alleyway.

BEFORE ATTENDING TO HEEKYUNG, Hyeri stopped behind a tree in the park and called Dongwoon.

"Hello?"

"Dongwoon, I know where the Soul Eater is."

"You had a vision?"

"Yes. It's at Keundolsan National Park."

"What? No way..."

"Yeah, what a coincidence, right? Tomorrow's shooting location is at the same place as a soul-sucking monster from another dimension."

"So what are you going to do?"

"Show up for work, scope things out, and try to figure out a way to kill that thing before it takes any more souls."

Hyeri heard him sigh.

"I'm guessing you're going to want my help…"

"Well, yes. How else am I supposed to kill it?"

"Ugh, and here I thought tomorrow was going to be a nice day…"

"I don't know what tomorrow is going to be like," Hyeri said, "but be prepared for anything."

"Gotcha."

She hung up the phone and went back to Heekyung on the bench.

"I'm sorry," she said. "That took longer than expected. Ms. Oh needed some help finding a shop and then she just talked and talked."

"No, I'm sorry," Heekyung said. "I have to go. I've got a really bad migraine."

"Oh no…"

"It's a long day of shooting tomorrow so I should rest before that," Heekyung said. "But thank you for a lovely day today. Really, it was nice."

He handed her the two unfinished ice cream cones and then he quickly left before Hyeri could convince him otherwise. As she watched him go, she vowed to herself that she would protect him tomorrow. She would protect everyone.

At least, she hoped.

Seven

It was early in the evening, a few hours before the shoot. The perfect time for a quick workout before he had to go to film. Heekyung started up his treadmill, feeling good. He would just go for a light jog before work, to wake himself up a bit more. He hopped on the slow-moving treadmill and started at a brisk walk to warm up. After a minute he turned up the speed, now speed-walking along. He meant to turn it up once more, to start his run, but he suddenly felt dizzy. He kept going at his quick-walk pace, trying to push through it, but the feeling only got worse. He quickly turned off the machine as white spots danced in front of his eyes, and he sat down on the floor.

What the hell was wrong with him these days? Why was his body betraying him like this? He kept telling himself it was just stress, but he was beginning to think otherwise. Ever since he saw that weird light that night.

Ever since that crack appeared in his bathroom mirror. Ever since he started seeing strange shadows in lonely places everywhere he went. Something weird was definitely going on. But what could he do about it? Call a shaman over? The press would have a field day with that one. He could see the articles now. "Lee Heekyung thinks his house is haunted." "Lee Heekyung going crazy." No, he would just have to deal with this himself.

Katalk. Katalk.

His phone chirruped from the kitchen counter. He carefully got up off the floor and headed over to it. When he opened it, he saw there was a text from Hyeri.

Good luck today! I know you'll do great! See you at the mountain. Below was a sticker of a Shiba Inu with cheerleading pom-poms.

Heekyung smiled as he looked down at his phone. He knew by now that he really had feelings for this girl. Just a simple text message from her was enough to make him forget his worries. Skipping his workout, he instead changed into his clothes for work, still smiling. Tonight was going to be a good night, he could feel it.

THERE WERE ONLY a few cars parked when Hyeri arrived at the filming site. She had wanted to get there early just in case something happened. So far things seemed to be normal, but she knew how quickly that could change. As she exited her car, she was greeted by none other than Ms. Han.

"Oh, you came alone," the actress remarked. "I would have thought that you'd arrive with your lover."

"We're not lovers," Hyeri told her.

Hyeri didn't have time for this. She needed to get to the site and make sure everything was okay. She went to move past, but Ms. Han stopped her.

"Oh, that's right," the actress said. "Because that would mean you're equals. And you're not. You're nothing but his little bitch."

"Takes one to know one," Hyeri replied.

Ms. Han's facial expression changed from one of smugness to anger.

"What did you just say to me?" she asked, her tone threatening.

But Hyeri was no longer afraid of her former boss. After dealing with ghosts and monsters, she could handle one snooty actress.

"You heard me," Hyeri said defiantly. "So why don't *you* stop acting like a bitch all the time and get over yourself?"

Ms. Han's reaction was swift. She said nothing, but raised her hand in response, and Hyeri was sure she was about to get slapped. But then another car pulled up beside them and Ms. Han lowered her hand.

"You're going to wish you never spoke to me that way," she said, then she left Hyeri alone.

Dongwoon had a slightly worried look on his face as he exited his car next to Hyeri.

"Is she giving you trouble again?" he asked.

"It's fine," Hyeri replied. "She's the least of my concerns today."

"Right. What if more of those people show up?"

"I think we'll be fine as long as Heekyung's around."

"Why's that?"

"Last time, the soulless person wouldn't come near him. The same thing happened yesterday when we were at the market. I think he must have some kind of power like us."

Dongwoon raised an eyebrow.

"You went to the market together yesterday?"

"Yes, just as friends."

"Sounds to me like you have a crush."

"I do not."

"Sure..."

"I do not! Besides, that's not important right now. When we get a break, we need to figure out where the Soul Eater is and kill it."

"Right. Just as long as it doesn't make me late for my scene."

"Alright, I'll tell the monster to be quick in its dying, for your sake."

"Let's just get this over with."

THE FILMING CARRIED on long into the night, during which Hyeri couldn't detect anything unusual. It wasn't until they took a break to eat that she noticed an expressionless person standing at the edge of the woods. The person hadn't noticed her or Dongwoon yet, so they weren't in a frenzy. They were just staring blankly at the film set. Then, as if receiving some unknown signal, they turned and walked back into the woods. Hyeri quickly made her way over to Dongwoon.

"I saw one of them," she said to him. "In the woods. We should follow him."

"Now? But it's so dark out."

"When else are we going to get a chance?"

"I was hoping we could wait until the filming was over."

"What if something happens before then? What if the Soul Eater makes a grand appearance during filming and we have to fight it in front of everybody? You want to risk exposing our powers?"

"I guess not."

"So come on, let's go."

"If we go off into the forest together, people are really going to talk."

"What's worse? A dating rumour about us or being known as Mr. Superhero to the whole world?"

"Alright, alright, let's go."

The two of them slunk away into the woods, trying to find the zombie man. The area was somewhat illuminated by the bright set lights, but they still couldn't seem to locate the figure.

"He couldn't have gone very far," Hyeri said.

When she received no response, she turned around to discover that Dongwoon was no longer there. Great, so they had gotten separated already. Even better was when she tripped over a root and stumbled into a rock pile. Hyeri winced as she tried to pull her foot free and found that it was stuck, wedged between two big rocks. She heard a twig snap from behind her.

"Dongwoon, can you give me a hand?" she asked before she realized that it wasn't Dongwoon behind her.

It was Ms. Han. The actress sneered at Hyeri's predicament.

"My, my, getting it on with all the actors in the show?" she asked. "I would have never guessed that you'd be such a slut."

"It's not like that at all," Hyeri retorted as she tried to wiggle her foot free.

"I mean I guess I should have known. Why else would all these handsome men be interested in a girl like you if you weren't just giving it away for free, right? I bet you even do it with that cameraman you're always talking to."

To Hyeri's horror she noticed the zombie man stumbling through the trees nearby.

"Now is not the time," she snapped. "Can you just help me?"

She locked eyes with the soulless figure and the man's

expression changed. He now seemed very interested in her and was coming nearer. Ms. Han followed Hyeri's gaze and smiled devilishly.

"Oh look, you have another admirer," she smirked.

"This isn't funny. Help me."

"I wonder if this one has a knife too. Ah well, guess we'll find out later."

Then to Hyeri's shock she turned and left, leaving Hyeri alone to face the zombie man. No longer distracted, Hyeri turned all her attention to getting her foot free. She twisted it mightily and with one final painful push she was able to pull it out. She limped as quickly as she could away from the soulless man, hoping to put enough distance between them that he would lose interest and calm down. At least until she could find Dongwoon.

It wasn't long until she spotted him, up ahead on the trail, looking oblivious.

"What the hell was that?" she exclaimed. "Why would you disappear like that?"

"Disappear like what?" Dongwoon asked. "You were right behind me. Weren't you?

"No, I wasn't. I got my foot stuck and almost became a meal for that soulless person!"

"Oh. Sorry."

"This is just great," Hyeri lamented. "Why do I have such a useless power? You get to have two strong, useful techniques and I get what? Seeing shit I don't want to see. And I can't even do that right either! It's not fair!"

At that moment, a black feather floated down from the sky and hit Hyeri on the head. As soon as the feather touched her, she had a clear vision of the Soul Eater. She knew exactly where it was now. She saw the rift it came out of too, at another location.

"I know where it is," she told Dongwoon. "Come on, it's—"

She was interrupted by a shout down at the filming site. It was that shout that let Kiha disappear back into the shadows in the trees above, unnoticed by the pair of them, a fistful of black feathers clutched in his hand.

"Hey! You can't come in here!" one of the crew members was yelling. "What are you doing!"

Hyeri and Dongwoon hurried down the path toward the filming site. There were now dozens of zombie people wandering around. Hyeri scanned the area for Heekyung but couldn't see him. Without his presence the soulless victims had free rein.

Then it happened. As if on cue all the zombie people suddenly turned their heads toward Hyeri and Dongwoon. They just stared at them, open-mouthed and expressionless.

"We need to go," Hyeri whispered. "Now."

Before she had even finished her sentence, the soulless people began to come at them, faster than they had ever been. Hyeri and Dongwoon took off running up the mountain path. Up ahead was an old temple with a walled courtyard. As they neared it, the gate to the yard mysteriously opened of its own accord. Hyeri didn't have time to wonder how that happened as the two of them quickly ran inside and shut and locked the gate behind them.

Bang!

Bang! Bang!

The sound only grew worse as the zombie people kept on coming, more and more of them banging on the doors.

"Why haven't they lost interest?" Dongwoon asked. "They can't see us anymore. They should be going away, right?"

Bang, bang, bang! Bang! Bang!

"I don't know," Hyeri replied. "Something's got them in a frenzy now."

"What do you think they'll do to us if they get through?"

"I don't want to find out."

"So what should we do?"

"I'm not sure. Can you use your power?"

"I don't know if it'll be enough. There're so many of them now."

Hyeri didn't know what to do. If Dongwoon's power wasn't enough to stop these people, then how would it ever be enough to stop the Soul Eater?

Her thoughts were interrupted by the appearance of a familiar silver-haired young man. Now Hyeri knew why the temple gates had opened for them.

"So, do you have a plan?" Haru asked as the banging on the gate grew louder.

"If you know something, just tell us!" Hyeri replied, but Haru simply shook his head.

"I'm sure you can figure out something if you work together," was all he said.

Hyeri was about to get angry with him for being so cryptic when suddenly the banging outside stopped. She looked through a crack in the door and was shocked by what she saw. She quickly unlocked the gate and threw open the doors. There was Heekyung, parting the crowd of zombie people like Moses parting the Red Sea.

"Come on," he said. "Follow me."

Carefully, Dongwoon and Hyeri walked out into the crowd. Hyeri took Heekyung's hand and the three of them walked un-accosted back onto the mountain trail.

"We need to get out of their sight," Hyeri said, and they began trekking further up the trail, Heekyung leading the way. Haru stayed behind at the temple, out of sight of the soulless people, but away from the others as well. He was highly suspicious of Heekyung now.

The trio finally stopped when they reached a small viewpoint, all of them tired and panting.

"What the hell is going on?" Heekyung asked. "What is with those people?"

"Um, well..." Dongwoon started.

"They're victims of a monster called the Soul Eater," Hyeri explained as Dongwoon looked at her like she'd gone insane. "It's a creature from a parallel dimension that got into our world. Dongwoon and I have special powers and we're trying to stop this monster before it sucks up any more souls."

Hyeri could see the apprehension in Heekyung's eyes. She knew he was doubting her story, as would almost anybody. He probably thought she was completely crazy.

Lucky for her that was the moment the Soul Eater decided to rear its ugly head. With an otherworldly cry it appeared in the air in front of them, flapping its moulting wings menacingly. It was horrifying to look at, like a giant misshapen bird from hell. It had a large black head sitting atop its lumpy feathered body of which two yellow eyes peered out. Instead of a beak there was a distended, gruesome-looking mouth full of rotting, festering teeth.

"Now do you believe me?" Hyeri asked.

Heekyung said nothing as he just stared at the monster in fear and shock.

"I got it!" Dongwoon yelled, and he blasted the Soul Eater with his electrical power.

It didn't seem to do much though as the creature just shook off the sparks and flapped its wings angrily.

"Do it again!" Hyeri shouted and Dongwoon held out his hands and let out another burst of bluish lightning bolts. It seemed to slow the creature a bit but didn't stop it.

"It's not working!" Dongwoon cried.

Again and again, he shocked the monster, but it

wouldn't die. It was beginning to come closer to them now, gaining a bit of ground after each shock.

"Why is he only aiming at one of them?" Heekyung asked.

Hyeri didn't know what he meant. There was only one creature there. Then she thought of Heekyung's mysterious power. What if there was more to it than just repelling soulless people? What if he could see things that others couldn't? Well, Hyeri had that type of power as well. Maybe she could see what Heekyung did too.

Concentrating all her energy, Hyeri tried to focus her power. She looked over to where Heekyung was looking and then she saw it, faintly. It was like another version of the Soul Eater, charcoal black, without any light or discerning features. It looked like a living shadow. Could this be the real body of the monster? Its "soul," perhaps? Hyeri didn't have any time to waste. The monster was almost upon Dongwoon now.

"Dongwoon! Over there!" Hyeri yelled. "Aim there!"

She ran up and grabbed on to Dongwoon's arm. Then she guided him toward the real Soul Eater. She concentrated all of her energy into helping Dongwoon. If this failed, then they were done for. The monster was already distending its disgusting mouth, preparing to suck out their souls.

Luckily Hyeri's intuition was right. There was a great flash of light as Dongwoon's electric power collided with the shadow version of the Soul Eater. The flesh and blood version let out an ear-piercing shriek as electricity also engulfed its body. It shook for a moment before exploding in a shower of black feathers and sparks. Hyeri watched in awe as wispy blue lights flew out from the exploded body and travelled down toward the city below. She suspected they were the devoured souls flying back to their owners.

"We did it," she said, breathily and gave Dongwoon a weary high-five.

Neither of them noticed Heekyung watching them with interest, his dark brown eyes now pitch-black.

"I'm exhausted," Dongwoon complained.

"Great job!" Hyeri heard someone say from down the trail.

It was Haru, looking happier than ever. Kiha trailed behind him, looking gloomier than ever. They were a stark contrast in both expression and colour scheme, Haru's silver looking bright next to Kiha's all-black ensemble.

"I knew you could do it," Haru congratulated them. "But there's still the rift to close up. Any idea where it might be?"

A sudden thought dawned on Hyeri.

"You can't see them, can you?" she said.

"What?"

"The rifts. You can't see them. That's why you need me to find them for you. Guess I'm not so useless after all, huh?"

Haru smiled at her, although she could see that it

wasn't genuine. There was a hint of annoyance in his expression.

"You're very clever," he said. "Let's just go find the rift, shall we?"

"Heekyung should come to," Hyeri said. "He could see the Soul Eater's real body when we couldn't. He might be able to find the rift faster than me."

"I don't think that's a good idea," Haru cautioned.

"Why not?" Kiha asked. "She may be onto something."

"He's not the heart," Haru told him and Kiha made a dismissive noise.

"We should make sure anyway," he retorted.

"What are you talking about?" Hyeri butted in. "What about 'the heart'? Will you please just explain to me what's so important about the rifts? I'm tired of all this secrecy."

Haru looked over at Heekyung who was watching them all calmly. The actor's eyes were back to their usual brown.

"Let's find the rift first," Haru said. "Then we can talk."

"Come on," Hyeri said, and she took Heekyung by the hand. "You're coming with us."

As she grabbed on to him, she had a quick flash of a vision. It was so fast she didn't really see it. But she felt it.

Terror. Pain. Darkness.

It was just like her dreams. It only lasted a moment, but it chilled her, nonetheless. She looked at Heekyung desperately, but his expression hadn't changed. He obviously hadn't felt what she had.

"Where are we going?" he asked her.

Hyeri didn't know why she suddenly felt scared of him now. She had never felt this way about him ever. But no one else seemed to notice what had just happened. Maybe it was just a part of his power she reasoned. Maybe he had visions too, and this was just an extension of it.

"There's one more thing we need to take care of," Hyeri told him.

The group climbed the mountain path together until they reached the site of the rift. Normally Hyeri would have enjoyed holding Heekyung's hand, but this time she had let go as soon as she could. It just didn't feel right. But the task of finding and closing the rift and the prospect of learning more about them had kept her from voicing her concerns. She just wanted to get this over with already and finally know what was going on.

"There," Hyeri said, pointing to a stone marker. "It's over there."

It was still fairly small and thankfully not growing bigger like the last one. Still, Haru seemed anxious.

"Hurry and close it," he said and Hyeri nodded.

She held on to Dongwoon's arm and he let off a blast of electricity as he aimed toward the rift. Things seemed to be going smoothly until Hyeri felt a hand clamp on her shoulder. She turned around to see Heekyung staring back at her. Only it wasn't Heekyung anymore. His eyes were pure black and in them Hyeri saw the darkness from her dreams, the one that terrified her to her very soul. She had no time to react as suddenly the great energy from the rift flowed through her and Dongwoon and into Heekyung. There was a bright flash of light and then all of them were knocked to the ground.

Hyeri winced as she picked herself up out of the dirt. That had definitely hurt. She looked over at Heekyung. He was writhing on the ground, his body twisting and contorting. It seemed as though he was fighting against some invisible force.

"What's happening?" Hyeri asked.

She looked to Haru for guidance, but all she saw was worry on his face. Kiha seemed agitated as well.

"It's one of them," Haru murmured in disbelief. Then he turned to Kiha. "You have to kill him. Before it's too late!"

"What? No!" Hyeri shouted.

She watched as Kiha obediently unsheathed his sword, but Hyeri stood between him and Heekyung, unwilling to let the demon past.

"Step aside," Kiha said.

"No. I won't let you kill him."

"I have to. I'm sorry."

"No."

"Hyeri, please," Haru said. "He doesn't have a power like you and Dongwoon. He's holding in a creature from another world. A world full of nightmares. You can't let it out."

But Hyeri just shook her head. She felt herself close to tears.

"No, you're wrong," she said. "He's good. He's a good person."

"The human may be good, but the thing inside him is not," Kiha replied.

"Please," Haru implored. "We have to kill him before it's too late."

Hyeri began to cry now. She couldn't help it. Heekyung was such a lovely person, she couldn't bear to see him die. Not when she hadn't even expressed her feelings for him.

"You can't," she told Kiha tearfully.

"H-Hyeri..." Heekyung's hoarse voice rose up from the ground behind her. "Listen to them... Whatever it is... I don't want to be responsible for letting it out into the world."

"No," Hyeri said, unwilling to believe what she was hearing.

"Please," Heekyung pleaded. "Don't let it get out..."

Hyeri only cried harder at his words. But she knew what she had to do. Although every fibre of her being was telling her not to, she finally stepped aside to let Kiha past. She turned away, unable to witness the horrible act. There was no comfort to be found with Haru. There wasn't a shred of empathy on his face as he watched on. Instead Hyeri went to Dongwoon who surprised her by putting his arm around her.

Kiha loomed above Heekyung, his sword at the

ready. Then he swiftly brought it down into the human's chest. But before it could pierce the heart, it stopped suddenly. Kiha tried to pull the sword back, but he couldn't. A thick black goo began to envelop the blade as Kiha looked on in horror.

"We're too late," he said. "It's too late!"

He watched helplessly as the human's eyes turned black. Then an eerie, malevolent voice came out of the human's mouth.

"Hello, world," it said.

The black goo pushed Kiha's sword out roughly, sending the demon stumbling backward. It then receded back inside Heekyung's body before a dark entity suddenly flew out of Heekyung's chest and disappeared into the night sky. Hyeri hadn't been able to make out exactly what it looked like. It had been just a ball of darkness. But somehow, even just looking at it, terrified her to her core.

Kiha sank to his knees in shock.

"Nooo!" Haru screamed.

It was a scream full of rage and frustration. And he whirled on Hyeri now, his eyes shining a bright electric blue.

"Look what you did!" he shouted at her. "Look what you did, you stupid human!"

Hyeri had never seen him look so fierce before. It frightened her far more than Kiha ever did. Haru grabbed Hyeri by the shoulders, tearing her from Dongwoon's comforting arm, and he shook her.

"Do you have any idea what you just let out!" he yelled at her. "The consequences that this will have!"

Then he grabbed the silver chain around her neck and yanked on it, breaking it like it was nothing. He pulled the sun pendant away from her.

"Wearing this, like you're actually fit to," he went on.

"Haru! Enough!" Kiha growled, and he pushed himself between the angry god and Hyeri. "I think I should be the one who decides who wears it..."

For a moment it seemed as though Haru might turn his anger toward Kiha. Then his blue eyes changed back to brown. He put the sun pendant in Kiha's hand as he walked away, defeated.

"Alright, I've had enough," Hyeri said, her face still streaked with tears. "Now one of you better tell me what the hell is going on. Right now!"

Haru just nodded grimly, ready to give in.

"The reason the two worlds collided," he said, "is because a god from our world was killed by creatures from another world. There is another world that exists next to ours. A terrifying one full of nightmares. The creature that was inside your friend, that's where it came from. The powers that you and Dongwoon possess are the remnants of a fallen god's power. You're 'the eyes'; Dongwoon is 'the hands.' There may be a third person, 'the heart,' who can help us close the rifts for good."

"My power... is from a god?" Hyeri asked, slightly in awe.

"Yes."

She didn't have time to think about that as she heard a groan from down on the ground. It was Heekyung. He was still alive! Hyeri went to his side immediately. He didn't look very good. There was still a wound in his chest, and he was deathly pale and seemed to be in pain.

"I'm sorry," Hyeri told him tearfully. "I'm sorry I couldn't protect you."

"D-don't be," Heekyung replied, breathing hard. "You did the best you could..."

"Well, my best was crap."

"Hyeri... there's something I need to tell you."

"Don't... Tell me when you're recovered, okay?"

"I don't think I can."

"Just hold on, okay? We'll get you some help."

She couldn't think that he would die now. She didn't even dare to let the notion enter her head. But she didn't know what she could do for him. Then she saw someone coming up the trail. It was Minki of all people. He didn't seem that confused about what was going on, just regarding the situation with a serene look. He walked steadily toward them, almost as if he was in a trance. He didn't even bother to say anything to Hyeri and instead focused on Heekyung lying there on the ground. Without a word, Minki knelt down and put his hands on Heekyung's chest. A bluish light emanated from his palms and then Hyeri watched in wonder as the wound in Heekyung's chest disappeared.

"I'm sorry, I can't stay," Minki said to Hyeri as he wiped away her tears tenderly.

His voice didn't sound like his own. There was another voice in there too, just beneath his own, a feminine one.

Hyeri didn't know what it meant, but then she heard Kiha from behind her.

"Please," the demon said, his voice choked with emotion. "Haneul…"

He came forward toward them, but before he could reach them a ball of bluish light floated out from Minki's chest. Then the light quickly flew off into the night sky, just as the dark entity had done.

Minki looked at Hyeri, blinking, confused.

"What just happened?" he asked. "How did I get here?"

Hyeri didn't know what to say. She was too relieved at Heekyung's recovery. All she did was give Minki the biggest hug ever.

As Hyeri hugged Minki, Haru went over to Kiha.

"We'll find her again," Haru told him. "There'll be another chance."

The stars in the night sky twinkled above the group as each revelled in their joy and endured their sorrow.

<hr>

HYERI SAT NEXT to Heekyung's hospital bed, worrying over him. He was being kept in the hospital just for observation. The wound in his chest may have closed up, but he was still suffering from stress and exhaustion.

And being a celebrity meant he was treated with much more care than the average person.

"Do you need anything?" Hyeri asked him and he shook his head.

"I'm just glad you're here." Hyeri smiled at that, but Heekyung's face remained grim. "But I'm worried about that monster," he said. "What if it has something terrible planned? It's all my fault."

"No, it's mine," Hyeri said. "I couldn't bear to see you killed. I…"

She stopped herself, not wanting to burden him even further by expressing her feelings for him. He had been through so much already.

"I imagine I'd choose the same if the situation was reversed," Heekyung said. "I didn't get a chance to say it before on the mountain, but… I like you, Hyeri. A lot."

She felt her chest being squeezed tight, like her heart was in a vice grip. He'd actually said it. He'd actually confessed first.

"I like you too," she replied happily.

The air felt heavy between them. This was it; this was the perfect moment. They were both safe, and no one was going to die, and Hyeri knew she should just go for it.

Hyeri leaned in as Heekyung did the same. She prepared for their lips to meet, but then someone was coming through the door. It was Minki and Dongwoon, arriving at the most inopportune time ever. Hyeri pulled away from Heekyung, slightly annoyed.

"How are you feeling?" Minki asked, oblivious to what he had just interrupted.

"Much better than before, thank you," Heekyung replied.

"No problem," Minki said with a smile. "I still don't really know how I did it though."

"I told you," Hyeri said, "you have godlike powers, like me and Dongwoon."

"I still can't believe that," Minki replied. "But still…" He touched a scrape on Hyeri's arm and watched as the wound miraculously healed. "This is pretty cool, I'd say."

HARU WATCHED from the hospital rooftop as the sun began to rise over the horizon, tingeing the sky with pink. He supposed there were still some beautiful things in this world. Although not many.

"Why do you care about this world so much?" Kiha asked him.

"My sister would have wanted to protect it," Haru replied. "You of all people should know her protective nature."

"And you of all people should know I can tell a lie when I hear one."

Haru just smiled at him. That fake smile that could easily charm humans but didn't work so well on a demon. Kiha didn't bother to ask again. He knew the true nature of the god and had his suspicions about why he favoured this world. Instead, he left and entered the hospital, going to check on the humans. He saw Hyeri in the hallway and approached her.

"So, are you ready for the long road ahead?" he asked her.

"What do you mean?"

"Fighting monsters, closing rifts. You know this isn't the end, right?"

"Well, I'll just take it one day at a time."

"You'll have to make some hard decisions, like killing someone you love, if you want to save the world."

"Look, I'm not some big hero trying to save the world. I'm just trying to protect those in it. When the time comes, I will always choose those I love."

Kiha was amused by her response. He was so used to the grand gestures of gods and demons that he forgot how simple humans could be. It was refreshing to hear.

"I think you deserve this," he told her, and he placed the pendant in her hand and closed it.

Then he left. As Hyeri opened her hand, she saw it wasn't the sun pendant. It was a moon-shaped one. She didn't know exactly what it meant, but she had a feeling she had just grown closer to him. She placed the pendant in her pocket and then carried on to the vending machine to get sodas for everyone.

When she returned to Heekyung's room the early morning news was on. They were recapping the incident on the mountain. The report was far from the truth, calling it an event of "mass hysteria," but Hyeri supposed that was for the best. If people knew what had really gone on up there, if people knew about the existence of monsters, there really would be mass hysteria. The report was over now and the next one came on. It was about a girl who had gone missing recently. Hyeri felt a chill when the girl's picture appeared onscreen. It was the one-eyed ghost girl from the market, the one who had asked her for help.

Hyeri looked over at her friends.

"I may not be a big hero," she thought, "but I'm going to try and make this world safer, for you, and for everyone."

About the Author

Mana Lee was born and raised in Canada but spent most of her young adult life travelling around the world. After living for awhile in Scotland and then Japan, she finally found her true home in Seoul, South Korea. It was there that she fell in love with the language, culture, and entertainment, and received the inspiration for her novel. You can find out more at www.mana-lee.com